This book was written for anyone who needs to read it, and published because of the astounding, unending support of those in my life, particularly my father. I wouldn't have made it this far without you.

THE CALL

M. QUINN

THE TABLE OF CONTENTS

Chirosapiencidae
"Trillers"

Strong hearing (esp w/ Trill reflection)

Head

bat-like ears

*Pointed snout-nose

large eyes take in light

NOTES
- reproduction occurs externally
- meritocracy
- Art in bioluminescence.
- Age: birth tree
- Naming Ceremonies!!

Note paper + fabric making } flattened pulled woven

DEVELOPMENT / AGE

ridged Shoulders

torso

coarse hair

*flat arms in here

* Porous *
* Contains Pancreatic System*

Pelvis

Arm
1
2
4 joints/ limb
Arm is longer than leg
3
Movement goes outward
4

Leg
Used to climbing rock surfaces
1
2
4

Foot

HAND
A
B
B
B
B

INTERNAL
Internal balance system

excess water   muscle

water is moved

Arthur Keene

THE CALL TO
ACTION

CTA 1

"It is the nature of Man to want all. Whether it be all knowledge, all wealth, all power, he wishes to have a distinct grasp on all that surrounds Him. This is how gods are born in the minds of Men, but also how they fall. When all of the power he has granted to these divine beings does nothing to help Him, Man will instead seek to become his own god. Armed with faith only in what He has, and a burning desire for what He does not, this is how Man advances."

[Angela Gallows, In the Minds of Mankind]

ARTHUR

My name is Arthur Keene.

1

I have spent almost my entire life in the First Impact colony on the planet Janus-CV197. If that name means something to you, then you may be a scientist, anthropologist, or have access to a newspaper. Either way, you know that there is a story to be told, and I'll be the one to tell it.

You have to understand some things. First, I really didn't know what would happen. Second, it wasn't an impulsive choice. There was no epiphany or sudden moment of change. You have to believe me. As far back as I can remember, I have wanted, deeply, to change the world.

I have spent most of my life being pushed and pulled around by forces greater than I. I have been shoved across the galaxy and shaped into one person after another by more powerful hands. The greatest force would likely be my father, Ace Keene, the space explorer. It was his hand on my shoulder through the walk from my mother's apartment to the ship, and from the landing site to the colony.

There were three weeks between those walks. Those weeks were spent among the stars. On Earth, space looks like a brilliant, flat, poster. As with most things, the truth is terribly, gut wrenchingly incredible. It's very difficult to stare into it as it surrounds you and not be reborn.

Some part of my life had ended on Earth. The final ties to my home planet were snapped as we move into the colony-buildings of plastic and metal standing as harsh slashes against a violet-tinted sky. The wispy clouds were unable to conceal the red shine of its suns, shifting a rose-tinted lens in front of my view. If I really focus, I can still feel the heat of the surface and make out a row of dusty green stalks rising against the curve of the horizon, stretching farther than I could measure.

Then I was inside the colony, away from the sun and sky, the green of farms, and the stars clear above me. Suddenly, I was in the world of screens and silver and the constant hum of machinery. It wasn't just around me, though. It was all throughout me. The air I breathed was half-recycled. The gravity under my feet was man made, or a third of it was. And just down the arm from my shoulder sat a hard lump . There was metal right below the skin, ticking and tracking my blood and my heartbeat and I didn't know what else. Everyone in the colony had a chip; they'd put it in a few days after we arrived. I cried for hours that night, but not because it hurt.

I was the only person there who hadn't volunteered to be shot straight off the surface of the Earth. I hadn't volunteered to go to a new home a galaxy away, on the first planet where humanity had found, and planned to live beside, a truly intelligent species. I also happened to be the only child who lived there, which left me no option but to grow up and learn fast. Back then, my father was a hero. at the time, he was mine.

There were two other men who had explored space with him. Together, they had discovered the planet. He claimed the glory, as he was inclined to do. Back then, I'd just assumed he'd done more.

The three of them were nicknamed "The Supervisors" by the other members of the colony. In my mind, the men will always be made up of shadows, harsh laughter, loud voices, and tobacco smoke. My father always laughed and smoked and boasted with them, leaving me with the others; the engineers, the scientists, and the researchers. Though I craved a guiding figure of any sort, the people who had time for me never seemed to stay for long. But I sat and listened and learned, out of sight and out of mind. I didn't do much, those first few years. I read and I cried, because I missed my mother, and I wandered the halls. I had a room, but I didn't spend much time there. If someone was looking for me, they'd look there, and if someone was looking for me, it was rarely for a pat on the back.

It's not because I caused trouble, I'll clear that up right now. Me and my hero just weren't anything alike. I was more like my mother- too much like her.

I'll talk about that later.

As the years passed by, my social skills were only getting worse. I didn't need them. I had access to all of the knowledge that the Planetary Union had to offer, and I devoured it. A hand-me-down screen and the smoke-damaged books from the library- I was never without one or the other. There was nothing else to do, and I hadn't had the joy of knowledge dragged out of me. I read as much as I could. Books on philosophy, language, math, science-fascinating science-and whatever I could challenge myself with. I tried to learn to cook, but was shooed away. I stood in the greenhouse and tried to grow a vegetable garden, but nothing came up besides a mess of weeds. Sometimes I sat with the workers in their common room, but rarely understood the references they made. Still, people smiled when I spouted facts, and knelt next to my spot in the hallway to read the spine of whatever book was in my hands. That was something to do, and something good, but it was exhausting. Worse, it was boring. My days had no difference, nothing I did changed anything, weeks and months blended together as I felt the sameness overcome me.

When I was thirteen, I still hadn't spent any time in a structured classroom, and I avoided any subjects I didn't like, but the researcher of the month believed strongly in proper education. He helped me find a GED prep program, running alongside the colony access lecture courses. Habitat colonies had high schools, research colonies didn't, though they had a full range of college courses. It was a major selling point towards becoming a colonist as a young adult.

I threw myself into it. It was hard, but it was new, and I just kept going, aching to be better. I didn't much like math, or analytics. I liked seeing problems, and solving them. So, as I drifted towards proper pre-college, I found myself drawn to anatomy, poring over holographic autopsies and improvised surgical tools. By sixteen, though, I grew bored of dense notes and useless certificates. I put aside the mass of traditional study and turned onto theories, abstract ideas, religion. There was no church on Janus and no logical reason for one, with the ideals of religions only loosely upheld even by those rare followers on Earth. The only real faith that could be found here was that of the aliens, the Trillers.

Known formally as Chirosapiencidae, they lived in mines, in farms, and some in stone huts. I could never get out of the colony to see them, but something about their world had a hold on me. It drew me to the windows whenever my mind wandered. I had seen broadcasts of the creatures, who looked bat-like, with large, luminous eyes and long, sweeping fingers. There were very few broadcasts I was allowed to view, but that drew me closer. Something had to be wrong. I was rarely worth the effort of hiding things from. I had done as much research as possible, yet it seemed to be the one subject that I couldn't access. I should have known the patterns mankind makes. I blame myself for not knowing.

At least I tried. Pointlessly. I threw myself into the search, spirits falling when my attempts fell flat, one after the other. That was the worst, even worse than the dullness and sameness. And then it turned again into the same mundane routine. I woke up, I worked, ate just before or just after the shift changes, read and wrote and turned into a uniform-gray smudge.

Eventually, frustrated with failure after failure, I shoved my tablet off of my table and stormed out of my spot in the library. I was restless, so I abandoned my usual haunts and instead wandered until I found myself at the research labs. What I came across that day, it set me on the path that has defined my life since then.

The large room looked empty, fluorescent lights reflecting off of stainless steel tables covered in electronics and lab equipment. The scientists that normally filled it with conversation and the white noise of work were most likely off on their break or in another lab. I paused a step inside the doorway, waiting a moment. Then, I turned to leave, my anger and frustration cooling. What followed still is burned in my memory, and will likely always be.

A soft movement sounded and I spun, my gaze landing on a creature that was so strictly, notably, fascinatingly otherworldly that the air stuck in my throat and my mind struggled to match it to something I already knew. Neither of us moved for at least twenty long seconds.

Just like the ones in the broadcasts, the creature's face was mainly taken up by large eyes, dark, with no iris. My stare was met instead with large pupils surrounded by a pearly ring of white. His face was decidedly masculine and coated in a fine layer of dark hair, which slicked back along a sloping forehead that ran into large ears. Their ends were twitching slightly, showing his alarm. His small, turned up nose looked like a blunt snout and seemed pasted on above a dark mouth. Thin lips curled back to show rounded teeth, with long canines shining pearly in the harsh lighting. Nothing in his features reflected my own, but he still looked achingly, desperately human.

My stillness must have shown that I wasn't a scientist, nor was I anyone with an intent to hurt him, or really any intent at all, because the Triller stood to move to the edge of his plastic habitat, revealing truly wild limbs. "He" moved in a way I had never seen, in all my research. His quadruple jointed arms seemed to unfold from lean shoulders, draped with a rough brown cloth that caught on the ridges of bone poking from his arms. His movements came from a place deep within, the motion radiating out to his limbs and resulting in a grace not seen anywhere but in underwater creatures. I'd read that octopi had been thought to be other-worldly.

I raised my hands up to show the hopefully universal sign of peace and sat in front of the plastic enclosure, noise-less. My knees were too close to jelly for me to stand. All thoughts were swept from my mind as quickly as they formed. I watched in awe as the Triller stood, legs as jointed as his arms, but oddly, shorter. His feet were bare, showing four toes, one more than the number of long, reaching fingers on each of his slender hands. His head came up just about to my chin. At the time, all of this information was but a passing observation, lost behind overwhelming shock. The creature's lips parted as it let out a low sound, the noise bursting from the back of his throat as he rested all three of his long fingers against the wall.

Obviously, I threw myself away from him. The noise was the kind that has all your cells telling you to run, seeming to explode from the same place his movements did, and linger in the air as he stared at me expectantly. And then, it struck me; this species was intelligent, so they had to have a language.

My brain started working a mile a minute. The next time he repeated the noise, I bolted. To be more clear, I ran at top speed to my room and returned with a pile of notebooks and a tablet, shedding papers as I slid around corners. I had to teach him my language, and now.

There was no time to waste. I was bored, I was tired, brimming with teenage angst. I'd read all my books, taken classes that did nothing for my future. I didn't play with toys, I didn't have a job, and no one talked to me. I was itching to live, to do something of literally any consequence, to fulfill the most natural human need for change.

I won't make it sound like a good experience. I'm not a great animal expert like Jane Goodall or Howard Letnard. I'm the one who sat and repeated the alphabet a dozen times, and pointed wildly at photos as I chanted "rock. Rock. ROCK." Of course, I'm also the one who cheered into an almost empty room when I figured out how to say "rock" in another language. That isn't a more flattering image.

I spent a week working every hour I could, hiding when I had to. I wasn't afraid of the scientists, but other fears tempered the thrill of discovery.

His name was Navelon (nach-VETCH-lu-hoan). I called him Ve or Vvvech. He was a significantly better teacher than I was. Still, by some miracle, he had begun to learn the chaotic patterns of basic English. Ve trusted me with his language, a gift like none I have ever received. Still, I struggled to push out the low syllables of his alphabet. It had an equivalent letter to all of ours, except C and J, which were made up for by three extra sounds that I had no dream of making properly. I did learn their shapes though, grasping a pencil the same way he did.

It was a language of mining creatures, and it was clear that the words were meant to echo along tunnels and bounce off rocks. Strong. Powerful. The world shook with them.

I took notes on everything, and had about fifty words, which I'm sure I wildly mispronounced. But Ve seemed satisfied with each of our grasps on the other's language. With our basic form of communication, I asked questions, and we shared cultures and information, talking like first graders on a playground. Each answer I managed to get from him just brought a thousand more questions to mind, but there was one that rose above the rest. I think it's best described in the journals I kept at the time.

"Day 7 of Trillian Communications- I want to know how they reproduce, what sort of technology they have, but

above all rises the question of Why. Why is he kept in a box? Why has nobody tried to talk to The Chirosapiencidae? He can't tell me, he knows so much less about humans than I do. Though, I am now realizing how truly little I understand us. Them. He talks of horrors, far beyond that which a Stone Age society is able to overcome. His culture, his people, they're taking them... Maybe he doesn't understand the miners. I refuse to believe that explorers and thinkers would place industrialism ahead of xenobiology. Too many variables.

Reminder: figure out how to discuss more abstract topics than good or bad. Top priority-Interspecies communications and Advancement.

Personal Note: I think we're friends."

[From the "Journals of Arthur Keene"]

It had been a while, or what felt like a while to a sixteen year old, and the thrill of discovery had faded into a comfortable curiosity. Visiting the labs was now part of my routine. In fact, I almost felt as if I was one of the scientists, doing things that mattered. I'd started going at night too, wedging the door before it locked and keeping my flashlight in my pocket. I'd move softly and cautiously on my way there, but I often raced back to my room, rushing to to throw myself onto my bed in a buzz of new words and realizations. I usually dropped my notebooks under my bed and properly shelved them in the morning. There were six of them, with short covers and creased papers. I'd had them for years, finding a new one when I needed it and filling it steadily with pen marks and ripped papers. Before I began each day, I would put them away, in a particular order and always just right. That's how I knew that one was missing.

I searched my bed, my desk, shook out my blankets, and felt panic rising in my chest.

The lab. It had to be in the lab. I hadn't brought it anywhere else. That was fine, I reassured myself. It was early. Hopping about on one foot, I pulled on my slacks and laced up my boots, my stomach twisting inside me. The walk wasn't short, but I'd taken it enough times that I wouldn't lose myself in the hallways.

The halls felt far narrower than they were supposed to, especially as empty as they were. I passed a few scattered workers. They ignored me, and I did the same. Things were looking good; I'd rounded the last corner and there it was, three doors down.

Two doors down.

One door down.

And I was face to face with the door, reading "Lab B;Organic" in black print on a white label, about an inch above my eye line. I hooked my fingers through the grip, easing it open. I spotted the book immediately.

It was in a death grip between my father's fingers, the knuckles nearly white. My lungs folded in on themselves at the sight.

He saw me and turned. As he did, the trio of scientists he'd been speaking to retreated back to their workstations around the room, which was a smart move for them. He stepped up to me, and I found myself drawing away, struggling to make eye contact.

11

"What's this." It wasn't a real question, and I didn't have a real answer. "It's got your name in the front, Arthur, and they found it here."

His eyes pierced through my skull, and I dropped my gaze to his jacket. He didn't often wear full uniform off Broadcast days. I think he saw me focus on the medals, and he raised his free hand below them.

"You see this, Arthur? This is a uniform. It shows that there's a system that works in this colony. It shows that there are rules that we all follow. One of those rules is that you don't bother the scientists. I see you skulk around, reading. I know you're some sort of clever, and you know, you understand, that you aren't supposed to be in here. These are pages and pages of notes, too, so you must have been sneaking around for a while."

I heard a ripping noise, and a page hit the floor. He'd gotten mad before. He'd torn the posters from my walls, sent my papers flying. He'd shouted, and that was easier than the quiet that was holding his anger now. As his voice rose, the scientists behind him snuck looks at me. I felt my cheeks flame.

"I'm sorry." I was, though I didn't quite know why. I knew my stomach hurt. "I wanted to help. I'm not doing anything here, but I could do that, and no one else was talking to him."

"Talking to *it,*" he corrected. "It's not a 'him.' It's a beast, and a brute. You're in this colony for a reason, and that reason is not to fool around with alien shapes and sneak into darkened, unsafe labs. Those creatures are violent, they live to attack and kill. That's why we keep them in the mines."

He lowered himself a few inches, raising the notebook to my eye level. "I need you to remember that, got it?"

For the first time, that made me pause. It was wrong. Not morally, not ethically or debatably. It was just honestly, factually wrong, but he said it so unquestionably. Ve was over his right shoulder, but I didn't dare look at him as I spoke.

"But they've got words, I can show you the words, and you can...You can talk to them!" I had barely taken a step towards the plastic habitat when his arm shot out, blocking my path.

"Just stop, Stammers. Forget the language and stop trying to be an adult."

"Stammers" was what the other Supervisors had always called me, because my thoughts always spilled out faster than I could find the words. My father had never used that name before. He'd said other things, awful things, but never something that so firmly yet so offhandedly defined us as being on opposing sides. It placed the last brick in the wall I didn't even know I was building around myself, and I stopped, like I had a choice.

However, I knew that I'd started something during those secret meetings with Ve. I knew that something far bigger than I could guess was happening on the planet, knowledge that would remain in the back of my thoughts during the years that followed.

The next day, Ve was gone, the lab was locked, and I swore that I'd never forget.

CTA 2

"Despite all of the advancements that have been said to make Mankind "better," have any of them ever made us "Good"? When wielding the power of our own brilliance, we, as a society, have two choices. We can use knowledge to unite, or to control."

[David Vejo, Temptation and Technology]

Not everything changed that day. Soon, the sameness returned. I'd ended up spending more time in my room and had entirely stopped wandering into the common rooms, now filled with new staff who were uncharmed by a clever teenager. I'd grown away from studying in the library, establishing a routine that included properly joining one of the research teams. My Dad had pushed me to it a few months before I turned seventeen, citing that I had a responsibility to play "my part." I ate with the rest of the staff, and listened to them talk about Earth, or the other colonized planets, or complain about the food. They only spoke to me about work. I didn't think about the food, rehydrated or dull as it was. Sometimes, on supply days, it was different, or a new wing of the colony was built up a few days later. I didn't bother with the changes, but I did watch the ship as it landed, and as it left.

I usually left before the meal was over. The labs' automatic lights were dark when the breaks were scheduled, but I'd kept my flashlight, and I worked in peace. Sometimes I looked at the plastic cube in Lab B, but not often. After everyone had returned to their rooms, or the common room, or to smoke in the garage, I ended up at my desk or in the library. Not for long, as there was a poker game there every few days. At my desk, I journaled or studied until that night flowed into the next morning.

I didn't exactly have hobbies, the closest thing being reading or continuing my research of Trillers. I swear, underneath my bed looked like the wall of a mad detective, and I must have acted like one, sitting on the floor with scribbles and drawings laid out in front of me.

I was in this position when, on my nineteenth birthday, I heard a knock on my door and my father's gruff voice summoning me. He seemed hesitant. The usual swagger was gone from his voice and replaced with something closer to a childlike anticipation. Still, this moment of humanity was clearly fleeting, as I heard another, harder, knock. Things hadn't improved between us after Ve, we rarely spoke.

When I was younger, we'd spoken more. Mostly when he was mad. In a flurry of mild panic, I scrambled to hide the papers under my bed and jump to my feet. With barely a moment to put myself together, I pulled open the door, skidding back just in time to avoid being the subject of the next knock.

"You're nineteen!" the man outside exclaimed with maybe a bit too much enthusiasm, always one to state the obvious. I had no clue why he was so excited about it, and all of the social skills in the world wouldn't have prepared me for what followed.

The first shock was that he hugged me, a stiff, awkward motion. I'm not entirely sure that either of us knew what we were doing, as we hadn't given or received anything close to that clunky embrace since I was much shorter. I know this isn't the story that you want to hear, but this is one of the experiences of that day that is engraved into why I did what I did. He was rarely so…close with me, usually more into shouting from the other side of the room. As a general rule, he sent me a gift a day or two after my birthday, and the most entertaining time I had of it was trying to figure out whose room one of his helpers had grabbed it from. I think I may have stressed enough that his visit was not in my normal routine, and things went more off the rails as his excitement came back, and he grasped my shoulder. This was almost another gesture of familiarity. It would have been a proud, normal moment, had he not been using it simply to guide me into the hallway without a moment for a mournful glance back at the research I was leaving behind.

We were headed into unfamiliar territory, both literally and metaphorically, as I had never left the colony's boundaries and we were on a fast track towards the exit. At this point, one might wonder, why did I know the way to the exit? I may seem like a coward but I was a coward with plans. I was always attempting to fool myself when I considered leaving, but I was dragged along with that thought. Again, not simply a metaphor, my father's grip on my shoulder continued as fantastic motivation not to slow my pace.

For the first time in years with no glass in front of me, I again viewed the curve of the horizon, a row of dusty green stalks, stretching...they seemed more dusty than green and they hardly took up enough ground to make a decent crop. There were silhouettes in the fields- something, working. Something certainly not human. I knew all the people in the colony, from guard to gardener, each of them only a name or a face, but I *knew* them. I knew none of them were in that field, even before I spotted the figures' large, curved ears. It should have been a hint to me of the realizations that followed, the way their backs were bent as their long arms tended to the plants. Words crawled their way from corners of my mind, not in my own voice, but in another, meant to be pushed out and echoed. But they were barely whispered as they landed at the tip of my tongue. There still seemed to be a hint of a tremor in the pebbles tracing the path we walked, and a flicker of movement that rippled through the figures. The weight on their shoulders lightened, for a blink. And then I was torn away, back inside.

We were seated in a fast-moving vehicle, and I wasn't entirely sure when that had happened. Based on the expression on his face, and the driver's firm refusal to look at me, I could assume that I'd spent the good part of a minute with a vacant expression on my face and that my father literally had to sit me down in the vehicle. I was already craving my notebooks. Curiosity is rocket fuel for the mind that can handle it. It sent my thoughts speeding through my head as fast as the scenery outside my window sped past. As far as I could tell, it was mainly rocks and dust and low, shrub-like trees.

We hadn't been moving for long before the motion suddenly stopped. His excitement was back, and my curiosity had in no way diminished, so our pace was fast as we headed toward a small stone building. I spotted the other edge of the farm bare yards away and took a moment to see the figures closer, my suspicions rapidly confirmed. And yet, the pattern continued, as I was barely able to comprehend this before there was again a grip on my shoulder and I was pulled along to what I figured was the point of the whole excursion.

And it was. A grin broke out on my father's face as he stopped, releasing my shoulder to throw his arms wide. As I watched him, the gesture seemed a little self-indulgent, reminding me of the circus masters I had seen in old videos. The moment of near joviality rang out loudly. Then, I looked ahead

Below us, the ground gaped open like the dark mouth of a sea monster, the teeth formed from jagged ridges of rock that circled down into blackness. It was like the twisted wreck of a car crash, rendering anyone who viewed it unable to look away. I squinted, focusing on the movements closest to the surface, and the crash turned suddenly into a six-car pileup. I had known that the planet was full of rich materials and had a strong magnetic core that turned Earthen technology into useless scraps of metal. Somehow, I hadn't didn't put the two together. It hurts to remember that.

There were Trillers, hundreds of them. A handful filled each ridge, digging and clawing at the rock. The workers a pale reflection of what I remembered of the species. I could hardly hear the frail trills that echoed up, rising as weak echoes out of the void. The surface was sandy, sandy brown and rust red, bleached from the relentless gaze of the sun. As the rock darkened further down, the miners turned to shadow. On each layer, tunnels branched out, like dozens more mouths. The miners marched straight down their throats in an exhausted defeat, head down and pace slow.

The sunlight beating down on my back barely penetrated the darkness of the pit. It seemed like a being from out of time, a malevolent one, ready to swallow you whole. Each miner seemed used to its oppression, their backs bent under its weight. No life could have prospered. The grace was gone. All had been forced out of them, replaced with something weak and growing weaker, wilting and dying. There were tall shadows thrown across the stone of the tunnels, dying torches turning the dark spots into another pack of menacing guards, watching over from some other realm. I was horrified, but as I turned my head to my father, his features betrayed no horror or regret—his eyes, in fact, gleamed with pride. My ribs froze and shattered in my chest, burning where the sun couldn't reach. I hadn't wanted to be the only one of the us with any morals. This was an intelligent species, with language and culture and society! And yet, here, they had been reduced to tools, pickaxes that the colonists didn't have to wield themselves.

My father's gleeful expression was somehow a more horrific sight than my new realization and something behind my eyes began to burn and sting, so I dropped my gaze to my feet. Next to me, in front of me, behind me—my surroundings were a display of callousness and greed. I hadn't ever felt anything so intensely, and my heart could hardly stand it. It pounded against my shattered, icy ribs and echoed in my ears, moving quickly to join the noises of the mines and push through my limbs. I felt my stomach flip upside down, and heard it groan in protest. I only half remember, but I know that my knees buckled and dropped until they hit the ground, dry grass gently waving around me as I gagged into the brush.

My eyes were squeezed shut and my fingertips dug into the soft dirt, soil sticking under my nails. He was talking. My ears were ringing louder. This realization isn't about me, though. My brain was far too scrambled to even consider putting together a rational thought, but I knew what was happening.

I knew it and I hated it and I'll say it:

It wasn't a research colony.

The man whose blood ran through my veins was profiting off the subjugation and suffering of an entire tribe of intelligent species.

I'd even been working there!

But it wasn't about me.

God, they were smart, and civilized, and just the scale, the heartlessness-I bent forward, laying my head onto my closed fists, hovering an inch from the ground. I tasted dust, and I swear I almost felt the pounding of the pickaxes through my slacks.

He came up behind me, and I claimed heatstroke, the shock clouding my thoughts through the ten-minute drive to the colony. The man was talking the whole time, but the words, spoken so cheerfully, washed over me. A phrase or two stuck in the back of my mind and echoed between my ears.

"Finally yours."

When we arrived back at the silver buildings, I ignored all laws of civility and silently found my way back to my room. As the lock clicked, I collapsed onto my bed. I squeezed my eyes shut, tears leaking out and staining the bed sheets. More than the horror was the despair. It was just so, so wrong. There had been wrong things before, but they'd ended up getting lost in the sameness. This wouldn't.

I had never encountered a problem I couldn't solve. In fact, I'd relished new problems, new challenges, anything to keep me from boredom. But this, this was a problem no mind could solve. If there was any solution it was in an army, and all I had was myself. That had been fine, before. Just me. I had known I was alone and prided myself on my self- sufficiency, sometimes tried to glory in my isolation. These "skills", along with my ability to remove myself from my emotions, were like a security blanket for me. Now, with one morning's events, that security had been torn away, and everything was crumbling around me. But it's not about me.

I allowed myself a moment of self pity. Curled in a fetal position on my bed, I let silence fill the room as a struggle started in my head. I felt the two sides of my brain tear at each other- rational and emotional. As if I was on the edge of a precipice, I clutched my hands to my head, attempting to shut everything down, attempting to return to the familiar and the rational.

It was safe there, behind my wall of facts, away from my emotions. And with the common sense and the clarity of that choice, I knew that I was not the one that deserved pity, and despised myself for figuring that I did. As my father mentioned in his ramblings, a change had occurred. But I hadn't become a man, I already was one. What had changed inside me was something entirely different from anything he could've guessed. Any trace of family loyalty was gone. I had no desire to take over the mines, to exploit the species. I refused to. I wouldn't grow old and greedy. Either the mines would be gone, or I would be. It wasn't a possibility or a goal, it was an unarguable fact. Simple enough; something was seriously broken, and I would fix it.

I'd never been told I was special. Certainly not by my father, but not by my mother, either. She'd told me that she knew I could make the world a little bit of a better place, if I tried, but she really believed that about everyone. Herself more than anyone, I think. Nearly every weekend was marked by a protest or some volunteer opportunity. She was in a group of mothers who took turns watching each other's children. Whenever she made signs, she painted them. I couldn't read, but I loved the shapes of her Bs and Ws.

Sometimes she'd take me, and I'd clutch her hand or perch on her shoulders to see the crowd, and she'd always tell me when something changed. She'd always read out the headline and say the same thing: "Look at that, Arty, look at that. If enough people decide to do anything—" She'd carry me to the window, or I'd run over to stare out as she flipped on the porch light "Things get brighter." It was miraculous.

She really believed that, that people could do whatever they tried to. The only difference would be that I was completely and totally alone, no allies, no family— actively working against my only remaining parent. I'd been betrayed by him before, as much as any child might feel themselves betrayed by their parent. Few memories held me to him. One, maybe.

It was before Janus, before everything. It was on Earth. My mother was alive, and we were in a city, buildings stretching high above us. They rose from the ground, towering like nothing on Janus. Everything was so much *more* on Earth. I watched myself reach up for the buildings, trying to grasp them in a child's fist. In my pursuit of them, I stepped into the street. I remember a car racing towards me, the lights growing larger and burning red and white into the back of my eyes. And then, my mother's scream and my father's grip catching me by the back of my shirt. The concrete grew close for a moment and I felt the car rush past. It was gone in a moment and a whiff of diesel. He carried me the rest of the way home and sat by me while my mother bandaged my scraped knee.

Then, she was gone. As he had been for most of my childhood, he was off in space during her last few months in the hospital. They were still finishing the colony set up, and he was there to watch. The city she'd grown up in was heavily polluted, and it had settled, finally, in her lungs. I mainly stayed with a friend, and I stopped going to school. I hadn't been good at it anyway. We left all memories of her in her old apartment, and all memories of my time on Earth. My picture books, soft sweaters, and my father's morals.r

I fumbled for more memories, but only found one, a clear mental image of a limp doll, a round, soft alien. It was in my closet still; each year I wanted to get rid of it, and yet it reminded me of who I used to be, of who I was. It was poorly patched—she couldn't sew—but it wasn't right to toss him out. I felt suddenly worse than when I'd first dropped onto my bed.

Finally, a purpose set me back in order. Silently, and almost robotically, I opened a fresh notebook and wrote a title, ready to organize myself, set myself on a course of action. I had a screen, but I liked using pens. There were none on my desk, but a bright blue one was on the floor by my feet.

I needed a plan. Something to do would get me going again, because it had to. If I allowed myself to stop, to rest, there would be no force great enough to put my brain back in motion again. I began writing. If there was ever a need for secrecy before, it had now increased tenfold.

A week passed before I gathered the nerve to plan a return trip to the mines. I had to see the real horrors, to accept what was happening before I could do anything to change it. Above all, I had to know if Ve was alive. If he was, I figured there were two possibilities; he'd either forgotten about me, or he despised me. The entire week before I returned, I didn't spare a moment to think, to contemplate, to dwell on exactly what I planned to do. In fact, I hardly paused to rest or eat, and instead I thought and I wrote and I planned and I researched. Everyone can take comfort in the usual, the known. Unfortunately, I was granted very little comfort past my nineteenth birthday. My father believed we had bonded, in some adult, masculine way.

My daily routine had changed. I found papers and pamphlets for me to read, left outside my door. And I got messages, too, following a similar topic. Each time I dared emerge from my room, I slipped into the hall like a frightened deer. Unfortunately, I was not a deer. When I heard loud noises, I couldn't run. These loud noises were generally laughter, the laughter of two...three men. Always, my mind flashed to the last sound to have put me on edge like that one did. I couldn't accept memories, I had to focus on facts.

That time, they were in the library. I shook the nerves out of my head, steeling myself again. Now that I had been exposed to their true business on this planet, I was expected to join them, or so I'd been told in a message that lit up mt tablet late at night. It really had been just a time and location. I had absolutely no idea what sort of bonding ritual I was getting myself into as I stepped through the library doors that first night. I'd sort of seen their meetings before, but I was usually kicked out. One time I'd had a glass thrown at me. When I slipped in, I caught myself scanning the shelves. They weren't really needed, most information was kept on computers or on tablets. The library was a formality, an exhibit, a place for them to smoke.

The entrance stood out from the silver-white wall, double doors of dark wood grain. The handles were brass, one tarnished. People only went in from one side, so only the right door handle shone from use. Shelves ringed the curved walls, each crafted from the same sort of fake wood as the door. The floor was a dark red carpet. I had once been fine, but it too had become faded. Dark green leaves curled out from stalks woven into it. I used to jump onto them, as if they could lift me up to the bright blue ceiling above. The ceiling was soft and curved as well, making the room look larger and continuing the theme of faux sophistication.

Natural light was kept on the other side of the wall, but fake windows mimicked Earth's sun. The center of the room was usually taken up by three dark tables surrounded by comfortable chairs, their legs embedded in the rug as after years of sinking in. Today, there were clear marks where one table had been dragged away between two shelves. There were wisps of smoke emerging from the top of the same shelves, rising in a twirling contrast against the cream-colored walls. I felt my resolve strengthen again. They saw no beauty in the ordinary, and no value in that which didn't come with a price tag. This was further evidenced by the dark smoke marks that marred the leather and paper of the books on the shelves.

Another round of laughter was ending as I slipped around the edge of the shelf. It took a considerable amount of effort to remind myself that I wasn't a child. I barely kept the tremor out of my voice as I put on a smile, weakly trying to project; "There's no need for the jokes to stop now that I've arrived."

The more they were talking, the less I had to. The less I had to talk, the less likely I was to throw up or faint from the pure effort of containing my contempt. The disregard and the hate and the disgusting superiority and their contributions to the draining and destruction and pollution of the world that had been given no choice in the matter. Yet, I smiled with as much conviction as I could muster, laughed harshly at their jokes. It dawned on me, that my father had never seen me in a moment of real joy. And how many moments of real joy have I ever had? It was another horrifying realization, in a week that seemed to already hold too many. It made so much sense, and yet still had to be impossible, that my sick, weak excuse for laughter could be seen as real by my own father. We weren't close, but still. Each night that I was expected to be with them, I was there. Each night, I laughed in my fake way, and each night, I left as soon as I could and returned to my work.

The week passed in a pattern of overlapping hate and disgust and repression. As it did, my molten anger cooled and hardened into steel, and the strength it lent me propped up my spine. "Make things right, make things right, make things right." The short phrase ran through my mind as more of a reminder than an encouragement as I left my room and my work behind. A handful of papers were clutched in my hand, and a recorder was jammed in my pocket. My heart still as I watched the scenery pass on my ride to the mines. I hesitated at the entrance, taking just a moment to stare into the deep gash in the ground. Then, I stepped into the shadows of the stone steps, the noises growing ever louder.

CTA 3

"Curiosity can be so many things to so many different people. A motivator, an instigator, a killer. It can be used to change the world, save lives, or end them. Even if the victim knows that the result is a tragedy, that will disperse no curiosity. Once the seed is planted, it is near impossible to stop its growth."

[Rick Mayre, The Cat Killer]

I almost lost my nerve as the sounds of the miners grew louder and louder. The darkness of the stairs was barely offset by gas lamps, proper lights made unusable by the magnetic core. The stone walls began to pull towards me, closing in as my breath came in short bursts. Waves of heat passed over me, and I felt sick again, lowering myself onto a stair. Doom washed over me, quickening my heart with each impact. Somewhere in the back of my brain, I was suddenly aware that in some dark room in the back of the colony, a screen was showing every time a beat skipped. The lump in my arm stung more than it had in a couple of years, but I had no free hand to clutch at it. The thought suddenly overwhelmed me that I didn't want someone seeing me panic, glancing at a monitor from some safe space. I wouldn't let them.

I was hardly a dozen steps down, and there was at least that number still remaining between where I stood and the entrance. I hardly allowed myself the luxury of a moment's rest before I forced myself back to my feet. This wasn't the first time my emotions had sprung up and attacked me like this, and I was facing enough without my mind turning against me.

I hadn't ever had a psychologist other than myself, so it wouldn't be the last time either. It felt like the sleep I'd missed the night before had suddenly come back to haunt me. I half fell and half lurched my way down. But I reminded myself of the plan, I had to stick with the plan. My determination grew together with my spite and the sudden hatred of my health tracker, and the toxic mixture steadied me. I was hoping to whatever people believe can cause miracles that Ve didn't hate me, because my plan hinged on his support. That, and being able to correctly pronounce the words I hadn't heard in years. There were a lot of risks involved, and I tried not to think of all the things that could go wrong.

By the time I got to the first entrance, I'd pulled my back straight and made my head as clear as I could. I clutched my facade of confidence as a shield while I slipped through the roughly hewn doorway. It was obvious at first glance that not a lot of humans came down. The bits and pieces of valuable minerals were being transported on a crude conveyor, a group of Trillers on each level scratching away at the useless rock around them. My heartbeat pulsed in my ears as I paced towards the first group. As they heard my approach, the Trillers turned. The footsteps must have been heavier than they were used to, despite the planet's low gravity. Though I lacked the grace they were born with, my steps were calm and measured. With all my focus on my movements, I nearly ran into a pair of workers. Their eyes went wide, almost wild, and they dropped the rocks from shaking hands, tools clattering onto stone. They spoke quickly, chattering. The rough words overlapped each other, and the noise ricocheted off of the stones. I couldn't understand all of what was being said, but the words were panicked, pleading. The chips broken off and discarded shook with the words, rising slightly in a trembling sort of movement. I stared for just a second before speaking

I had practiced the word for friend-ally. I repeated it slowly, and the was impact immediate. They stopped talking. Then they burst out in another round of chatter. Stepping away, I knelt, ignoring the noises and the miners creeping out towards the commotion. A sharp chip of rock in hand, I scratched letters methodically in the ground.

"A R T H U R" and then again in their own alphabet.

I paused, looking up and pointing at myself.

" F R I E N D. G O O D. H E L P" I drew slowly, first in English and then, more carefully, in the symbols of the rough mining language. Dropping the sharp stone, I sat back. I stared at the letters, the shapes engraved shakily in the slight layer of dust coating the stone. I had practiced the alphabet every day for a month after that day I found out that Ve was gone. I didn't dare to speak the words, even when everyone in the colony was asleep. However, I could write.

No one could stop me from tracing the deliberate letters of the alphabet in my notebook. With another breath, the noise faded, everything falling away as my heartbeat was the only sound in my ears. I wrote out the letters of Ve's name, the scrawl steadier than any other words I had written. Even when practicing every day had turned into once a week, a month, and even when the motivation had faded altogether, even then I wrote his name. In each of my studies, it had seemed too disrespectful to write his name in the language of the men that had taken so much from him and his species.

At the name, the Trillers went wild. They must have been stunned to know that I knew words of their language, but a specific name? As the clamor faded, a miner emerged from the small crowd. I looked slowly and…it wasn't Ve. Of course it wasn't. The miner was a female who pointed to herself and slowly enunciated, "Lough." Probably a nickname. Triller names were long, and sharing them with people outside of your colony was sensitive. Ve had been stunned when he realized I had told him my entire name within minutes of our first conversation. it wasn't until he'd shared his that I felt the importance that should be put behind it.

With Lough as my guide, I entered one of the branching tunnels and headed straight down the throat of the mine. The sounds of our footsteps echoed among the noises of stone hitting stone. The ceilings were low, sheltering, but the walls allowed two people to walk side by side even at their closest point. Though they were rough, the stones showed signs of once having been smooth, carefully tended to. The rooms were poorly lit; anything that couldn't be removed remained as jagged silhouettes. As we went deeper, the rooms were more full and unmined, though the fabrics I could spot on the beds were torn, and nearly everything else was covered in the same fine layer of rock dust.

It was tragic, the beauty and effort ignored. The circles of light showed walls marred with rough holes where small ore deposits must have been, the larger ones marking the end of each hallway. I caught a glimpse of the mines and a moment of clear trilling noises each time we passed a new entrance. What I could see in the few pools of light spilling from the small lamps was otherworldly. The conditions were inhumane; yet, even in the darkness and the oppression, the way the Trillers moved was so natural.

They had their grace down there, fingers sweeping the stones, casting long shadows behind them. However it sounds, I refuse to glorify this; my point is just that my father, and the colony altogether, could never break them. Even more than the injustice, my admiration of the species pushed me to the choices I made, all done in a struggle to earn the trust that this grand species placed in me.

I would never dare to say the long tunnels were a safe place, a comfortable place, or even a place that wouldn't remain as a feature in my nightmares. The feeling of defeat was soaked into the very pebbles that dug into the soles of my boots. The air tasted like metal and stone, pain carried in the cool drafts and words carried in the solid walls.

Thankfully, farther down the route, the holes were fewer, and the elegance of the smooth stone could be admired. It had been something carefully sculpted in a time before, carved into rooms and halls that the colony had made them destroy. It wasn't a luxurious style, but one made with care and effort. I could almost see a shadow of workers chipping away at the rough stones, the images fading from my mind as our pace slowed. I figured that we had to be getting close. Here I found that I was correct, and the pounding in my ears suddenly rose to a crescendo. We entered one of the larger hollows, and I paused as my guide strode faster towards the workers. It wasn't the lowest level. I took a moment to stare down into the remaining depths. This darkness was softer, a blanket instead of a cage. I let the sound of actual conversation fade as I stepped slowly into the hall, my focus trancelike. I could see more mines, but some of the others looked like they were lived in, or at least they used to be. I didn't dare to venture into the maze. Instead, I rested my hand on the smooth part of the wall, palm flat. I felt a vibration, like the chorus of many voices, and the many conversations of the workers seemed suddenly clear.

Just as quickly, I pulled my hand back, feeling like I had again taken advantage of an intimacy I did not deserve. I realized the conversation I had been focusing on had faded into silence. Taking this as my cue, I turned to the pair behind me, feeling the attention of four luminous eyes, and the pricking feelings of many glances. Word must have traveled fast, as something electric sparked through the air, the near tangible expectation raising the hair on my neck.

I'd planned for a hundred terrible possibilities, but not for this. I hadn't planned for the breath to be knocked from my lungs in a burst of recognition, or to feel suddenly young and scared and unsure. I'd grown taller, but his head still came to the same place below my chin. He looked nearly the same; features a little sharper, calluses and scrapes dotting his hands and feet, but a familiar face in an unknown environment. I saw recognition shine in his round eyes. I felt ice grip my chest as their corners narrowed with suspicion. Then, his expression relaxed as he pointed to me, speaking words that I wouldn't have understood even if I could've heard them above the roaring in my ears. Lough stayed by the wall, her stance defensive and her gaze trained on Ve as he stepped toward me, pausing just six inches away. The three years had aged him far more heavily than me, with lines creasing his face and dust lightening his hair. I watched his hand extend, but still found myself tensing away as it landed on the white cloth over my shoulder. He withdrew, and then laid his palm on my chest. I felt tears burn behind my eyes as he brushed the dirt off my jacket and dropped his hand to his side.

He spoke my name, gruffly, and poorly, and without the "th" sound, but he knew me. With that reassurance, a half dozen miners joined us. The tears had drifted from my eyes to my vocal cords, but I cleared my throat, as I had things to say.

I won't pretend that the speech I gave was awe-inspiring, or truly a speech at all. My words were slow, shaking, barely enough to get my message across. Yet, they still listened in dead silence. I spoke of how I'd just found out what was happening, and how I hated it and how I wanted, desperately, to stop it. The words themselves were basic, though they somehow still captured the attention of the workers, spoken with a hope and determination that echoed beyond the cavern where I stood.

The point wasn't to tell them that they should want change-of course they wanted change. It was just...After two decades, Better could still come.

If only for just a moment, I felt the connection that they must have felt, experiencing a moment of truly being part of something like I never had. I stumbled and I stammered and yet, there were no scoffs, no jeers, just a stunning amount of respect from those I hadn't yet fought to impress. There was a moment of silence at the conclusion, and the many gazes slowly turned back to their work, the sounds resuming their normal tune. Ve walked into the hall, and I followed.

My guide went back into the maze of tunnels, leaving us in a charged silence. I opened my mouth to speak, to defend my actions and promise I could change things. As I did, his hands raised, slowly, deliberately, and again, I couldn't keep myself from flinching away as his fingertips rested on my forehead. It was a gesture that felt protective, almost familial. Unlike the flat palmed contact of friends, or pressed foreheads of those in love, his simple movement showed a welcoming I can never claim to have felt from any past interaction, and hardly any since. And then, a simple word, mispronounced, a base response to my promises, my ideas, my plans.

"ha-ow?"

CTA 4

"Every species is guilty of it, an ideal lodged in the instincts of any animal with the intelligence to survive. Change must be halted, and those that are different must be feared. Different in mind, in body, in beliefs or language; they represent the possibility of danger. In animalistic society, these dangers are either expelled or exterminated. However, the "humane" approach of our society can be judged as much crueler than nature's treatment. To be cast into a life of mockery and scorn, of forced change and being molded if not judged to be useful. No creature born into the mold set for them has ever had so much to prove as those who don't fit. Whether they impress or not, succeed or fail, those born into normalcy can

find comfort in the mundane, success in the
mediocrity of a life lived. Yet, these poor,
unusual few are cast away, or judged only by
the value that they bring to the majority. Is
it any surprise that the runt will accept a
place in a human household, that even the
wounded wolf would limp to any offering a
semblance of welcome."

[Mia Dyran, The Runt]

The plan I had developed was, at its core, a terrible idea. I didn't have the power to shut the mines down, even if I eventually got control of them. Besides, I couldn't sit by and wait for my father to skip off to retirement. I refused to. Unfortunately, I had neither the ability nor the influence to complete my goal alone. Those in power back on Earth had to know about it, that wasn't a question or an uncertainty. That meant that they were ignoring the violations, or actively profiting off of them. Even as a child, I'd heard little whispers and jokes about the Union's corruption, so this was far more worrisome than surprising.

In a leveled ambassador system, or any sort of worldwide single government, abuse of power is inevitable. Even before the Crisis, the wealthy class survived on a different plane than the 99%, and the Supervisors must be a part of that class. If they could pay, they could influence. So, the people at the top weren't going to help. Still, they were elected up from each state and country, and needed support, so the majority—the many people not in positions of power—had a voice, if I could get them all shouting.

But there was a hierarchy in the colony, and I had not yet earned a high enough status to be able to send a comm down to Earth. Thus, I had to be smart. Not book smart, I had to be clever. I had to take my father's clearance, send a message as him. Or, that was the plan. I had to contact those on Earth that controlled the broadcasts.

That was step one. I also had to get out of the colony, to get a video of the abuse. That was easier thought than done, as the doors to the outside were locked at all times, and a patrol of guards made their rounds to keep out the planet's animals. When I was allowed a habit of going to the mines, one always joined me. They were lax though, grown lazy by a lack of problems, and my companion always lingered at the top. So I just had to find out how to leave without a keycard to open the door. I couldn't just walk out casually. With the guards at the door knowing I wasn't a supervisor, they'd stop me and send a message to you-know-who, and considering that part of my plan was to ditch him in a meeting room, I wouldn't make it to the mines.

I spent my time away from the mines and the library in my room, poring over a map of the colony to find some path that would keep me from failing the creatures I wanted so badly to be accepted by. Then, it hit me. Something I hadn't thought of because it made my already terrible plan so much worse. I had to blow out the power. There was a backup generator that kicked in after two minutes, so I'd have to get out before two minutes were up. The locks were electronic, so they'd be blown. The artificial gravity inside would be gone too, but the pull would be just a little lighter, and I'd begun practicing outside and in the mines when I could.

Since my role had been made clear—be a face and a last name—my time in the labs had gone way down, and the rules surrounding me had mainly been lifted.

I spent hours running the route from the generator to the exit. Hours and hours, until I could do it in the dark, which I would have to. I practiced more than I should have, using the learning as an excuse to procrastinate.

Running wasn't my only preparation, though. I spent hours teaching the miners how to humanize themselves for the camera. It is an unfortunate fact that humans are more likely to care about others if they're similar to themselves, because they care about themselves over any other species. And over any other member of that species. Ve had been spreading some of his base knowledge of English, to make communication easier. Mostly, they learned the words, "Help us." They forced their mouths around the sounds, turning the simple syllables into an eerie and unnatural chant.

I hated that I had to teach them this in order to make people care, but it wasn't me who infiltrated and managed to corrupt this culture, it would just be on me if that corruption continued. Good effort and a bad plan, this stood as my mantra as I went on my way to actually see the generator. The hallways were a dangerous terrain, with lights spread few and far between and guards on patrol along the route. I knew the route, I could manage the important bit in a minute and a half.

It seemed subterranean-more than a basement should. The basement was one of the few places in the colony that was geothermally cooled, giving it the smell of stone and copper. It was just a concrete walled hole in the ground, silent except for the humming of machinery. The white noise was somehow both comforting and unsettling. I studied and planned while I ate in my room, when I woke up, before bed. Every spare moment felt electrically charged, those weeks before.

I was a bit too on edge to actually enter the power room, but I knew how generators worked. Connect the positive and negative power flows and short it out. Simple. Less simple; I couldn't touch the conductor without being completely fried. Functioning on far too little sleep, complex engineering ideas eluded me. Instead, I decided to throw something long and metal to bridge the terminals. Just launch it wildly at something that could possibly explode. When the metal touched both contacts a huge spark would be created, and the chances of me dying were relatively low. I didn't care, I had no life to protect, and I was devoted completely to that cause, as willing to die as a soldier. Noble, but I would later find out that Janus wasn't the only planet suffering from environmental attacks, and efforts to change things are much more effective when the person making them is alive.

I was satisfied then, and moved on, the beast that resided in the power room still held back by sturdy doors.

Next was getting the message back to Earth. I didn't have close to the clearance that was needed to do that, which was an issue that I considered for a long while. I ended up with one question; who *could* send a message back? The supervisors. My father usually had his tablet on him, so he didn't bother with a password. Still, in order to take it, I'd have to distract him. He was a creature of habit, and I'd learned those habits to avoid him, so I knew where he spent his time almost every evening. Sometimes the men would pass out in the library, and I just had to ensure that happened when I wanted it to.

That night, I was in the library early, tracing my feet along the carpet's stems. The familiarity of the dark green lines steadied me—propped me up a little. The day had been normal, my plans had been made and finished, and I decided to return to the routine I'd had before. The people in the labs, they knew me, but they still stared when I wasn't looking. My skin prickled with the feeling of them watching me, and I just barely saw them out of the corner of my eye.

As soon as the men entered, I rose, the movement forcing any signs of weakness out of me. And as soon as they had sat, a great deal of settling was apparently necessary for the chairs they used five times a week. Maybe it just seemed longer than usual, every moment stretching past.

"Good news." I announced hoarsely. Not a single one of them looked up. "I may have…" I continued, voice fading to a weak whisper. Again, I reminded myself I was no child, I was no longer inferior. With a slight cough, I repeated my words, louder, their gazes slowly turning to me. Like a pack of lions they stared, deliberating on if I was worth the kill or not.

"I may know how to increase the efficiency of the mines," I began, my words causing no change in the faces of the men in front of me, itching to get to their drinks. "And increase the profits." In my mind, everything was falling to pieces. Then, there it was, a spark of interest. Letting out a sort of squeaky, nervous laugh, I continued.

"I'd love to explain tomorrow. First, we should celebrate the future."

The three of them shrugged, sort of, and cast glances at each other with no real meaning behind them. There were some mutters, but those faded into contented clinks as they collected their glasses. I filled them quickly, allowing the men to dissolve into their normal conversation. I couldn't hear a word. My heart was pounding in my ears as I forced my focus onto two tasks, pouring drinks and tracing the branches arching up to the ceiling, my eyes following the curving path. I found myself so on edge that I flinched at each particularly harsh laugh, each fumble for the bottle.

That was the first time I'd ever stayed through the whole evening, and I didn't relax until the bottles were empty and everyone was out cold, draped over armchairs or asleep on tables. I crept out of the library, even dragging my feet to avoid any noise as I slipped down the hall. Unfortunately, being quiet did not make me invisible, and I almost jumped out of my skin when I heard my name called. It was an effort to not look guilty as I turned around, and as my eyes landed on a man whose name I just could not bring to mind. Instead of saying anything, I silently opened and closed my mouth.

Thankfully, he talked instead, gesturing back down the corridor as he called, "Old men passed out again? I can go get them...if that's why you're here?"

Fumbling for my words, I laughed politely, closing the distance between myself and the door to my father's room. "D...don't." I called behind me. "You know how they are... when you wake them up...."

Fifteen seconds of mutual polite laughter later, he was gone and I was inside the room, hurrying to the tablet. I knew the comm-code, and I managed to get it to communications. I'd planned out a curt message, in his style. "New Development. Ready for broadcast on tablet 1182082118 at 0800 Eastern time tomorrow. Authentication code: 1351155145."

I pressed the button, the screen flashed green, and something solid settled in my chest. It was set in motion, and couldn't be taken back. The next day, I'd either save the species or...not. I might not. I might fail and throw the rest of my life away into suffering. I might live for years and years as a miserable, terrified man, alone on a suffering planet, my head ringing with the echoes of that pain. Acknowledging that didn't make me feel at peace, but it did something to alleviate the deep-set fear that clawed at the back of my brain.

My walk back to my room was uneventful, though my heart raced in my chest. Time had dragged by when there was none to waste, but now, it stopped. I had nothing I could do until the next day, and I wanted, suddenly, to do everything and nothing all at once. I stared at my ceiling most of the night, only managing to fall asleep two hours before I had to stumble out of bed. I had a schedule to keep.

I was in the conference room twenty minutes after I woke up, dressed in a proper colony jacket and all that which comes with the on-camera uniform. My only comfort remained that this morning was going to be a lot less pleasant for them than for me. I had the locks ready, my tablet in my pocket, and I was as practiced as I'd ever be. Adrenaline had already begun rushing through me, keeping me on my feet.

The Supervisors stumbled in fifteen minutes later, downing headache relievers with their coffee. After a moment of settling, I stood, my mouth suddenly dry. I'd planned to say something, but I couldn't bear it. "I...I'm sorry," I let my practice overcome my emotions as I grabbed a metal chair, hardly feeling the joints pinch at my skin as its form collapsed inwards. I was moving as if the hesitation could let me reconsider. They stirred, one almost standing. I ran to the door and slammed it closed behind me. The electronic lock clicked automatically.

It was as I was running, leaving the confused voices behind, that I realized I wasn't sorry. I pulled the chair over my shoulders and sped down the hall, the voices echoing louder. Counting down in my head, I felt my feet pounding the floor, pushing me down the hall. I couldn't stop. My brain was on pause, so my body had to keep moving. I started to hear more footsteps, other residents of the colony beginning to make their way towards the conference room. As I mentally thanked whoever installed steel doors, I slipped into the power room, the chair dropping from my hands in shock.

I hadn't gone in before, because that would have made my plan real. It would have meant seeing the beast and knowing that it would be waiting for me. Then, it was real, and looking at it made my heart stop, or skip a few beats at least. Icy needles of panic pricked my skull, my fingers, my chest.

The generator was encased in a metal cocoon, only a few symbols showing through a window of thick plastic. I could see no contact points as I had imagined, just an impenetrable case. Still, I threw my chair at the tarnished silver, mainly as a release of my internal frustration. Maybe, just maybe, I had the slightest hope that I could salvage my plan. Maybe I imagined that it still might manage to short out the machines and the power would be out with one dying buzz. The chair bounced off the shell and hit the floor, the noise ringing in my ears like a mockery of my false hope. I was crumbling, the adrenaline fading as my knees began to buckle, sending me careening towards the hard floor. It might be nice, the cool metal...I was burning up, suddenly and acutely aware of the echoes of voices growing closer.

It was for nothing. The hours of planning, and the years of learning before that. The caring, and the teaching, and every second where I'd actually thought I could do something to shut down the mines. I'd messed everything up. I should have waited, planned more, and he was going to be so mad.

He was going to shout and storm like he had when I was younger, and burst holes in my walls that posters never properly covered. I wouldn't be able to do anything for years, wouldn't be allowed to go to the mines. And in the mines...they'd keep dying, and it would get worse and worse and they wouldn't know what I did. They'd think I gave up on them, broke my promises. They'd suffer that much more deeply—because of *me*.

Then, as I hit the floor, I spotted it. A small control board, fastened to the base of the generator. Almost sobbing in my exuberance, I slammed my fist onto the reset button, all lights going black and the sounds of machines fading. The voices rose again, but I couldn't make myself care.

Two minutes until the lights were back on, and I could run my path in ninety seconds. My head was light and my feet were lighter, though that may have been due to shutting down the gravity controls along with the power. It was like I was outrunning everything—every monster in my head, every rude comment or harsh laugh, every injustice I had witnessed—they were propelling me towards what I knew I had to do. No key card was needed to open the door as I shoved open the clear plastic, taking control of the nearest vehicle.

This route was less practiced, but I had taken the trip enough to find my way. As i approached, the soft spots of light in the mine were visible, highlighted against the darkening violet sky. The broadcast was beginning, so I didn't have time to stop. I jumped out of the machine and rolled as I turned on the video, which was shaking as much as my hands. But that didn't matter. I spoke calmly, my voice clear as I hurried towards the mines.

"People of Earth, my name is Arthur Keene. My father is Austin Keene, the man that found intelligent life among the stars."

My voice had started to rise in volume, from my desperation, my emotion, and the clamoring growing louder on either side of me. In front were the mines, with echoing, shaking shouts. Behind me, the members of the colony had spilled out in a mess of waving arms and headlights and roaring engines. They'd left after me, but weren't far behind.

"This intelligent species, The Chirosapiencidae, they are being used as no more than tools. This wonderful, unknown world has been corrupted by greed."

I turned the camera to the crowds racing after me, squinting from the light on my own face. I could hear the Trillers in the mines, knowing I was coming. I could feel their hope in the stones that seemed to rise before me, their pleas in the trembling of the rocks. I wanted to answer the whispers, to shout the words that had been on my tongue for years. Still, I stifled them. My shouts would stand for freedom, which I hadn't yet brought them.

"We, as a species have failed them, failed the duty from which we claim the right to imperialize and industrialize beyond our own power. But, I plan to be...to be one of those who will fight to change this. One man cannot change the world, though. Will you help me, people of Earth?"

I heard my voice, and it was shouting, coming to the edge of the mine as the buzzing in my ears reached its climax.

"I'm not looking to wage war on those who disagree, as they are fools who deserve our pity and our aid, not our hate. All they have is hate, so all they give is hate. We will give them knowledge, and they will help us spread this knowledge to this species, first, and help us open ourselves to the many secrets of the galaxy. And, beyond that, we will spread the knowledge of self preservation and not ravaging our world for scraps and resources. This is not a war cry, it is a call, people. A call to action! To unity! To knowledge and...."

I had meant to say "love," but I couldn't. Not with the anger that shone clear in my father's eyes as he led the crowd of those following me. The cars had fallen back, as the ground may have collapsed under them. The supervisors and faceless guards hadn't been slowed by that, though. The scientists hadn't followed, or the researchers, none of those who weren't profiting obscenely off the suffering. Those in the middle of the crowd had their screen out, and my own voice echoed back at me from them, a beat later. I could feel them approaching, the rumbling of their steps louder than the chorus of hope. They were close. I spun, starting to face the camera towards the mines when it was forced out of my hands, the momentum sending me stumbling forward, my heart in my throat. I twisted, seeing his face, his fury, his silence in a scream that rose as the ground gave out around my feet, and I fell into darkness.

According to the Janus colony's health trackers, the heartbeat of Arthur Keene went flat at 0804.47, on March 15, 176 S.E.

THE CALL TO
RISE

CTR 1

"No matter where you find yourself... you would find a set of rules you must follow. Rules of life, of civility. Rules of nature and rules we each set ourselves in our own mind. By these rules we live and by these rules we claim the right to judge the actions of others. Our legal system is guided by the written and unwritten laws of our civilization, and juries in the "court" of our everyday lives deliberate on the rules of one's own morality. These rules are subjective, formed by each person's own choices and experiences. These are rules of life. However, these biased rules cannot be allowed in Law... The purpose of a legal approach is to display the facts of a situation to be judged against the rules of law and logic, not opinion."

[Nova Bale, Life and Law (academic paper)]

The Broadcast swept the news like wildfire. It started on Union channels, but was picked up by private stations just about thirty seconds in. Even magazines and newspapers had their turn with it for weeks after. The broadcaster, a young man named Arthur Keene, was called everything from "a hero" and "a martyr" to "a faker" and, very specifically, "a child propagandist paid to spread lies as a publicity stunt." Overall, even the critics called what happened "a tragedy." And it was a tragedy. Not the communication, or the way it ended, but the way the world reacted. Fan clubs sprang up. Stories and poems and a few trashy documentaries were written about him. Not one of them said a thing about the point he'd made, they just glorified and romanticized the death beyond recognition.

Tabloids theorized and analyzed, but very few people seemed to actually be willing to acknowledge the message he was attempting to send. There was nothing to be done, for most people. Not me. I saw those horrors he spoke about. Not saw, but listened, and understood. After all, he didn't manage to record photographic evidence, although that could be forgiven because, well, he fell hundreds of feet down a mine.

With everything we had done to the Earth—overfishing and poaching and polluting—you'd think people would learn to care. For weeks after, I watched people, combed the news and social media, and I saw no one doing anything that could make any impact. Again, not their fault. They were cowering because of the governmental influence needed to support such an immoral project as was described by the guy who lost his life in protest. People died and killed protecting secrets much smaller.

Everything had started out normal enough the morning before the Broadcast aired. I burned my toast, but found a good seat on the subway. My roommate and I had gone out the night before, and she was up later than I was. We'd been friends since childhood, and we worked together, but she was at a different building that day, so I rode alone. I listened to a radio show about bugs. There was a slight delay, but the office is just by the station, so it worked out fine. It's a law office-environmental law-run by the Union. I'd gotten the job straight out of college, with debts to pay. It wasn't what I'd expected, nothing world-changing, but it was the field I'd dreamt of.

Why? To start, I had the summer after I graduated high school to do what I wanted, and I'd headed from my home in Colombia to New York to spend some time getting used to the city before I started school. I was young and excited and set on a career in law, but my goal was general. I wanted to defend the innocent and punish the guilty.

While sightseeing, I found myself at the New York Aerial Gardens.

This wasn't surprising, considering it was one of the city's greatest attractions. The land had fallen into disarray during the early Crisis, but the city had paid for it's restoration in 111 S.E, following the popularization of casual gravity manipulation. At the entrance, the gardens didn't look like anything special, just a short concrete path out of the parking lot, and scattered ticket booths ringed with tall silver towers, all smooth except for the spheres topping them. The only sign it was a garden was the flowering bushes and lush green hedges. I adored any of the rare glimpses of nature left in our world. All that is lovely, but nothing particularly extraordinary. That came later. You had to buy a ticket before you were able to pass through, stepping into a surreal new world. Sloping hills sprawled out under a thick carpet of grass, winding paths of concrete and dirt disappearing into tunnels of trees, reaching above even the museum at the main entrance. It stood proudly behind a statue taken straight from ancient Rome, ivy climbing up the walls. You could walk for hours without repeat, stumbling on exhibits of art and spreading water features, or the more secret places deeper in the trees. Tiny worlds of flowering rose bushes or lilacs, the hidden space inside a willow tree's falling branches, or rocks piled just like steps, just like something Nature picked out just for you.

All of the beauty, even accompanied by the white noise of chipmunks chattering, birds chirping, and water flowing still wasn't enough for people who craved the truly surreal. So, if you were to take a moment to look up, you'd see why it's called the Aerial gardens. I was knocked back when I first saw them. The sky above the gardens is absolutely full of glass shapes. Spheres or cubes or pyramids, pointed or curved, clear or colored. They held their own climates, the plants inside ranging from cacti and desert flowers in colored sand, to all the wild blossoms the jungle could offer, sustained by tiny hydroponic pools. In some of the larger floaters, I could even spot reaching coral and the squat shape of sea anemones.

More commonly, a rainbow of wildflowers and weeds, garden variety sunflowers and daisies and dandelions, looking like something from another planet when they were framed just right against the sky. I spent my first hour there like everyone else, enjoying the sights and sounds, trying to catch some of the smaller floaters.

There was a community garden where I grew up, and people grew flowers on their steps and in their windows. I'd even grown purple wildflowers in a pot in my backyard to give to a girl for valentines day. That was different, though.

Unfortunately, I can never enjoy a nice thing, and it all began to feel wrong. The faces of the sunflowers were turning towards a sun that they couldn't truly feel on their petals. The lilacs were pressed against the curve of their container, petals breaking as they tried to grow. Even the ivy hanging off the edge of the open-topped spheres seemed like Rapunzel's hair hanging from her tower, a beautiful cry for help. In our terrible, unstoppable human arrogance, we had forgotten that we used to rely on Nature and instead forced it to rely on us.

It was then I decided to pinpoint my major. I, in youthful hope, really wanted to become a voice for the world we were destroying as we claimed to save it. We became so dismissive as we found our way into space, like an infectious disease that drained its host and moved on, allowing it only enough time to heal to be useful again. This may seem melodramatic and grand, but some things cant be said casually.

When the now-famous broadcast began, I was at work, in one of those steel giants. All around me was traffic and skyscrapers, steel and glass, overlapping phone conversations, and the smell of diesel outside open windows. These were as deeply woven into the city's roots as blood was soaked into the soil of the continent. It was why I loved the city, but also why I couldn't stand it. Sometimes hearing the city come alive at night made me want to come alive as well, and other times it made me want to slam the entire population of New York City over the head with a shovel, and then use that same shovel to bury myself. In the past, when you wanted to leave the city, all you had to do was drive until you hit the wilder parts of the state. But those days are long gone.

Short version: people realized they were living on a doomed planet. Deforestation, pollution, and poor land management left only scraps of the natural world, trapped in greenhouses or walled gardens. When they ran out of space, things started getting worse. Overpopulation, water shortages, poor waste disposal and people refusing to protect themselves from very avoidable diseases led to hundreds of thousands dead and a world of panic and war. They lived in chaos because our ancestors couldn't step up and deal with their problems and left them a wasteland of a world. Unable to save the planet, scientists started to search for others. That's how we evolved into an era of star travel and united ourselves in forced peace and definite corruption.

If people in the past had just put the effort into protecting their world, we would have had a proper one of our own. And we could have avoided the war and near-extinction, as well as the xenophobia that followed.

I consider that a lot, even though it's not worth considering. As they explored, they'd found other inhabited planets, from bacteria to dog level intelligence. As we spread out and began to intervene in the affairs of other species, and began to industrialize their homes, it became clear that our past had been forgotten. Or ignored. It was in good part due to our lack of biodiversity that Earth had shifted into the industrial wasteland it's become. The Trillers had no choice about what we were doing to them.

Thinking about it made me mad. Imagine if you could go to your ancestors and shout at them to stop. Just to stop all the destruction and pollution. It just wasn't something I could let go of. Thankfully, neither could my aforementioned best friend, Rosaline. Rosaline and I had gone to high school together and gone through two and a half years of college, with no break to travel or work in between. It's practically impossible to believe that people used to do four years straight.

The college experience, for the most part, spat out people with two things: degrees and debt. The debt became unsustainable and the degrees became unusable or unachievable, so now we take up to ten years with breaks between them. After two, however, we had a reason to go out in the world. We needed money. We were students, in one of the most steadily expensive cities in the world. And that's how we ended up at the job.

In the beginning, all was wonderful; I loved the people and the courts and the work. The city and its heights, the small shops tucked away in alleyways, restaurants that served near-perfect Metemgee or takeout Sancocho, the background buzz of people talking, a constant reminder that you weren't alone. After living in a house full of kids, I found the noise comforting. Until I didn't. Still, I kept on, unsettled as I was. That's not the point.

I had started the job to have a platform to help innocent people, the ones without a voice, anyone who needed justice. The firm, however, only seemed to be motivated to help a small percentage of people. The one percent. The Broadcast felt like a shining opportunity for us to branch out. For me to branch out, if I'm being honest. I wanted to scratch that itch that I'd been feeling. To rid myself of the horribly stifling feeling the city had been giving me. I figured that surely the Planetary Union would want to help another species in need; it was the dream behind space exploration. It was the dream painted on the posters, at least. After the Broadcast, I waited for someone to say something about it. A day passed and nothing happened. That made enough sense. People were probably in shock. Two more days passed, each hour dragging past.

Every day, I got up, got my coffee, listened to my music or my show on the way in, did my work, had lunch nearby, and then went home and watched the news until every cell in me shook with the need to do something.

Janus was too visible, I figured. Too trendy, too in the spotlight. Good idea to avoid getting involved for a bit. But after a week, I couldn't take it. I had seen flashes of the video or articles about it on everyone's screen at least once, but no one had said a word.

The work seemed dull and unimportant.

But, my mind argued, it couldn't be. I knew it was good work. Consider: Did this company pollute the air around its twenty- four factory locations? Yes. How much did they have to pay for the damage? I say all of it, but my job was to dig up stats and theoretical writings so we could convince a jury they shouldn't pay any of it. I hated it. I couldn't deal with it any longer. I was just tired of saying nothing that would make a difference, working against my ideals and against the things I cared about. I had to change. I was just tired of not living a proper life. I'd ignored social obligations and hobbies and all for years to get to where I was then, and I absolutely refused to accept that it was worth nothing.

I started looking around some more, combing through the comment sections of articles, joining chat-groups that had sprung up, digging in as far as I could. It was a little consuming, but I couldn't give it up. In one of the groups, I mentioned the office I worked for, and woke up to a new message the next day. One of the other members, a woman halfway across the country, was an organizer for a native protections group. And man, she was motivated. They'd filed a case for the Janus natives by the next afternoon, and there was just one more step for me to take.

In my mind, I would burst into my boss's office, alight with the flames of justice. In reality, my approach was much more timid, a few light raps on the door and a less than enthusiastic "enter" as a low energy welcome. My thoughts were buzzing with facts, and a planned-out proposal was forming and rearranging in my mind as I pushed open the wooden door, barely able to see his blurred face through the plastic window. His name was spelled out in overly grand gold-colored letters that had been peeling from the smudged surface since before I started there.

"Sorry to bother y-" I began, almost immediately cut off by the man's curt interruption.

"You waltz in here, distract me from my work, and now you haven't even got anything important to say." As the graying caterpillars on the man's brow inched together, my teeth scraped against each other, my fists clenched, and my breath came out in a low whistle. This could seem curt, but it's not a moment I view with a lot of joy.

The heel of my hand dug into my side, but I answered civilly. Now, I wouldn't. "I was trying to apologize, but that's not why I came in here. I was approached by a Native rights group about a case; the public will be on our side, and we can really help people."

I was really trying to keep up a non-challenging humility. That's what you have to do. The illusion of weakness was both my shield and my burden, and it would be worth it if I could get the firm to take this case. Three words into his reply, I began to drop my illusion of timidity, hardly able to handle the indignity as he slammed his palm against his desk, his pens scattering.

"You're gunning for my job with this, then. Aren't you?? There's no need to be aggressive!"

I brought my palm into my side again and pulled a breath through my teeth. My tone was even. Barely. "I'm not being aggressive! I need to say something!" I knew it sounded like a child, demanding permission instead of telling a fact. Still, I pressed on, because I needed to get to my point.

"They want to continue the work of that kid who's been all over the news, the one on Janus. The history of this planet is full of problems that stemmed from industrialism, and now that same kind of industrialism is beginning on another planet. There could be a whole species that needs us."

"No. That's not what we do." He said it as if I should have already known, and my face flamed. Even if I was too dense to realize he was sending me off, the act of returning to his work would have pushed me over the edge. I was getting more frustrated, everything I'd decided to "just deal with" and put aside was boiling up.

"What don't we do? Help people? That's why I got into this field; that's why this branch was formed!"

That was true. After the Crisis, it was clear that environmental regulations had to be put in place, to give the planet a chance of being habitable. Those needed to be enforced, legally, so they brought in trained prosecutors. It worked, for a decade. Then the offices shifted into a personal defense team for the businesses of high members of the Union, and protectors of whatever destructive projects occurred on government territories.

His tone was scathing. "That's a dream, nice to think about." The man was rising slightly from his seat, palms pressed flat to the desk. "We're here to earn money and win cases. Anyone who says anything else is either lying or trying to get a job. Though clearly, that failed for us both because we're here, stuck in *environmental* law."

His voice was low, angry, but he wasn't the only angry one. I could feel tears pricking the corner of my eyes. I didn't know what I should say, or even what I could say. I really cared about this job, needed it. I had convinced myself nothing that brought the peace the Union did could be so thoroughly corrupt. I had to believe that or I would never be able to drag myself out of bed in the morning.

When I spoke next, I was biting the inside of my cheek to stay cool. "I've wanted to be an environmental lawyer since I was seventeen."

"Why?" He scoffed, clearly never having had the epiphany I did. "We're the jokes of the law profession. I make just over 100K a year, I'm almost laughed out of my class reunions."

My anger spiked again, that someone could be so ungrateful for that great a position, that great an opportunity; it made me hate in a way I hadn't ever felt before. I felt venom rise to my tongue, and I knew it would poison me if not him. "And you're unhappy? How do you not know how lucky you are…you ungrateful, weak-minded, people pleasing coward!"

I was fumbling for words now, thrilled by the furious release. There were hundreds of thousands of people living in dumps from the plastic waste of the past, thousands more without food and water because people couldn't see how much they were taking, couldn't see there was an end to Earth's bounty. No one could seem to learn from the past, and it was infuriating.

"If you say one more word, you're fired." His pale face was a rapidly darkening pink, and a vein was bulging on his neck. He had to say that, had to show that he still had some pale shadow of control.

"I quit!" I found myself shouting, my voice seeming to echo in my ears as if I was watching myself from afar, no longer the one in control of my own actions. I couldn't deal with the job any longer, and being fired, while receiving unemployment, would leave a mark on my record that wasn't worth the pay. "I'm going to take the Janus case, and I'll see you in the High Court, and if you die before I complete this case, I'll see you a little lower!"

I turned and stormed out of his office, then the office, then the building altogether. I didn't know where I was going. I just knew that I had to get out and keep going.

CTR 2

"To have morals is a gift, one granted by a
cruel God, one that forces the best people
onto the hardest paths, and laughs as they
struggle with the threat of soul-corrupting
desires…To have a conscience is what makes us
human, but so is the ability to ignore it.
Animals know what they are supposed to do to
survive and do not exceed those needs by any
malicious intent. However, the human
conscience has cultivated a world where the
path to success is to ignore it."

[Joseph Wells, The Cons of the Conscience]

I had been home for a few hours before Rosaline came
through the door, windswept, with a box of my office sup-

plies falling apart in her arms. She said nothing. I said nothing. The silence hung over us like a cloud, lingering. I spoke first, alternately overwhelmed by waves of emotion and none at all. "I had to." My mouth was dry and my fists were shaking against my sides...I was scared. More scared than I had been when I quit. I was scared that she would look down on me, find another roommate, another best friend. I was nearly certain, just then, that she would see how angry I'd gotten and wouldn't be able to deal with it. I wouldn't have blamed her if she couldn't. I couldn't.

All she said was, "I know."

That was just about all it took to make me break down sobbing. I couldn't do anything else. So I didn't. She sat by me, silent support while I cried. She'd sat with me like that when my mother was in surgery and I couldn't fly home, when I'd had a bad breakup with a guy I thought I loved, when my cat died. In that moment, she was the only thing that kept my world from collapsing. The silence remained for another half hour, broken only by the shaky breathing of one exhausted after a night of emotional release.

Finally, she spoke again, "You know I can't quit. What they're doing is wrong, but that doesn't mean we should lose the lives we worked so hard to create over it." I knew she was right, as much as I hated the fact. After that, no more was said on the subject. She continued to go to work, and I started my job hunt the next day.

It was terrible.

Well, it didn't start off terribly. Friends from the office messaged me with questions and sympathy that made me regret some of the explosiveness of my exit. I didn't regret quitting, though.

I reached out to some old classmates, an ex-girlfriend I still spoke to, some former colleagues that went into private companies, and dug deep into job recruiting sites. I had interviews lined up every day for a week, and I felt refreshed, ready, determined.

Then that week passed, and I was beat. All the meetings had started off well, pretty much. But they all ended about the same way; with an uncomfortable silence at the mention of the Janus Project.

That weekend, I started to make a new budget, settling into the possibility of unemployment being my reality for a while.

However, I did have one meeting left, with a woman who had been friends with my favorite college professor. She'd reached out a few days after I'd quit, but had been out of the office so the interview was set later than the others. By the time the day arrived, I had dealt with failure and failure again.

I showed up early and ended up waiting by the receptionist. He was only a few years older than me and *gushed* about the office. He'd majored in English, but was saving up to go back to school to study law, and yes he had put up that customized calendar, thank you for asking!

We chatted for a few minutes, before he suddenly broke the conversation with a "Looks like Ms. Delnem is out of her morning meeting."

"Kora" I heard a voice behind me, turning to meet the kind gaze of a 50-something woman in a yellow blouse. "Hi, I'm Kora. Sorry to keep you waiting, Nova. Is Nova okay?"

"Nova is great, my full name hasn't suited me since high school."

"Anne—Professor Vida—mentioned. She also mentioned how hardworking you are, and we love hardworking people here."

I pulled my purse off of my seat and trailed behind her to an office with lavender walls and a clear door. There was no nameplate anywhere I could see, but there were papers and photos, or projections at least, in frames on the walls behind her.

"So, good grades, two years straight, two years experience, and you've published papers?"

"Two, yeah. One in a college publication and one in an anthology arranged by a friend of mine."

"Well, you really seem driven, and so are we. And you're okay with starting in a position that mainly focuses on research? For a short while at least, I'm sure you'll move up quick."

"Yeah, of course. I'm still helping prosecute the bad guys even if I'm just defining the proof."

"Great, all great. I can't believe they just let you go at your old job." I felt a spark of pride glow in my chest at the praise. "Speaking of your professional past, why did you leave the Union office?"

"I wanted to pursue a case, and in conversation about that case, I realized that I was unhappy with the integrity of the office."

"Well, the Union…" she trailed off, and I nodded solemnly.

"All that aside, what were the details of the case?"

"A Native Protections agency reached out to me when I was looking through information about—" The words stopped still in my throat. I didn't want to say it. After I said it, she'd say I couldn't follow the case, and then I'd be betraying my cause if I took the job. If I didn't say it, it wasn't the same betrayal. But I wouldn't lie, and I'd gone too far to pretend I didn't care about the project."—about the Janus colony. From the Broadcast."

"Oh." she winced, "you know, we can't associate with someone trying to prosecute them."

"You can't."

"No."

"I sort of figured." I felt a weight again settle down onto my shoulders.

"There are A-level ambassadors actively for it. Hawthorne for sure, but I heard two more back him silently. We're not small, but we aren't invulnerable enough to go against that kind of force. The job is yours if you want it, but you'll have to tell the NPO that you can't do what they asked."

I took a breath, dropping my eyes to the surface of her desk. I was so tired of the hunt, worrying about my savings. I was tired of being angry, and the office seemed so nice. I wanted to be doing something, even if I wasn't following the exact topics I'd intended. "I'd have to tell them I couldn't do it." I repeated slowly. I was working through the fact, drawing it out and letting the sounds hang in the air. As they faded, I saw her shift in her seat, the first hints of impatience making their way onto her face. "Nova?"

"I'm sorry, Kora. I can't ignore the case in good conscience."

"I really think you'd be a good fit, though. What if we made you a prosecutor? It's a higher salary, and you'll be in a courtroom within the month"

I wanted to accept so much that it hurt. But I couldn't. I'd quit because of the integrity of the Union office, and I was no hypocrite. Integrity is everything when you're against corruption. "I'm so honored that you'd do that for me, but no. I can't."

"Contact us if you reconsider."

"If I do, you'll be the first I tell." I wouldn't, and I knew it then.

"Be careful, Nova."

"Yeah." I slung my bag over my shoulder again.

I could have taken the job, been steady, or successful, but I'd be stuck feeling the painful itch that makes all passionate people want to change things, and not being able to do a thing to scratch it. Helping the creatures on Janus wasn't a virtuous choice, it was a deep need. I was tired, hopeless, close to giving up.

Obviously, I didn't. But money wasn't coming in from interviews, so I did have to get myself a job. I found a temporary position at a coffee shop, the one right down the block. I could walk there, and I recognized some of the regulars from my building or the ones nearby. The people were nice, and I got free coffee in the mornings and learned how to work a cappuccino machine. I liked to draw smiles on the recycled cups—nonuniform, crooked, and sometimes smudged smiles. There was a man with the sweetest dog; a blonde terrier whose collar matched his owner's signature leather jacket. There were a lot of odd customers, but they were mostly the harmless, comfortable sort of odd that you see around the city. Of course, not all of them could be. One man in particular left me with chills and the instinct to check over my shoulder.

He was undeniably unusual, everything about him. Unlike the normal coffee addicts and sugared-up aspiring writers, he was surrounded by an aura of cold confidence, his posture upright and his steps short and quick. It didn't seem like he was hurrying to get away from something though, more like he felt people should be running from him, spreading a path in front of him. They did, looking cowed by the harsh sound of boot heels hitting the cafe floor.

Imagine you're working at a second rate chain cafe and, amid the various sweaters and flannels, some man pushes through the door in a shroud of ice and cologne, with a half a suit and half a face. The right half of his face and his right hand stood out as startlingly unnatural. They were metal and laid out as harsh slashes against what would have been classic features. The eye glittered like ice, a faint silver, an almost human iris shining in the socket. An inch out in each direction, at least, his skin faded into scar tissue, the metal underlying slipping under the skin.

I'd seen poor prosthetics, but anyone who went around in with a gold watch on their wrist could've easily gotten a graft.

The noises of the coffee shop faded, and I was sure it wasn't just in my head. He beelined towards me, dodging around hipsters waiting to order. His voice was accented, which was even rarer than the metal hand he rested on the counter. It seemed as if he took pains to hide it. The voice, certainly not the prosthetic.

"Just a coffee." He spoke as if he expected people to pay attention. It seemed carefully cultivated and thought out.

"Name?" My voice cracked sharply.

"I'm here to offer you a position in higher government. Better than your old job. And definitely better than-" he looked around, lip curling up in disgust "-this."

"I think we need a shorter name. To fit on the cup." His laugh was cold, and fake. "Calix."

Calix's tone grew a little more insistent, and I grew a little more on edge. Still, any woman in business deals with insistent men.

"You'll have a better life. Just one thing…." As if I'd already agreed, he went on to qualify it. Cool and emotionless, matching with the robotic features scarring the side of his face. I began working on the drink, but he didn't stop talking. "We can't have people going against our money makers. One of those money makers happens to be the project on Janus. I've heard you're a very loyal person, so, I'm sure that loyalty can be brought to us when you come to work with us, and your side project can be forgotten."

His drink was a quick one, making it took a lot longer than it should have. I was fumbling for the words to respond. I knew what I wanted to say, and I put up my professional smile again. I held his drink out loosely.

"If you know I'm loyal, you should be able to guess what I'm loyal to. That'll be $2.75, not much less than the cost of your loyalty, I'm guessing!" I couldn't believe I'd said that, but I was mad and had been watching a lot of drama TV. Too much. He took the drink in a clenched fist, before he again seemed to fade into a calm, robotic man. "Passionate people are the bane of human advancement. You'll soon find how passion suits you outside of dreams, and you're not going to like it." There was a horrifyingly cheerful lilt to his voice, matching the skip in his step, each tap of boot heels against the floor echoing horribly in my ears. He didn't even drink the coffee, dropping the entire cup in the bin by the entrance.

I quit my job at the coffee shop the next day, after a night of research into the man who called himself Calix. Was I scared? No. Shaken? A little, yeah, obviously. Mostly, I was more motivated to take this case than I had been before. In my research, I didn't learn much. He'd clearly changed his name, it was too Greek for someone who looked like the Middle Eastern kids in the foster community I'd grown up in. I dug through other communities, figuring something tragic had happened to him. Tragic story aside, he was trying to intimidate me out of my ideals, and I had to focus on which A level ambassadors might be employing him to shut down my fight.

It had to be three out of the seven. Not enough majority power to reveal the project to the public, but enough to keep it going as long as it had been, almost twenty years.

Thomas Hawthorne, Elayne Monthale, and Henry Jian. All were near retirement and had moved up the chain of power the way they were supposed to. They reached the top and then stopped doing things the right way. It was all a rumor, but that was mostly because proof against you didn't really last long once you hit a certain level of authority. There was something seriously corrupt going on with these three politicians. Most of them were corrupt to some degree, everyone knows that. But, if it's between someone who strong-arms businesses and someone who profits off alien enslavement, its more worth focusing on the latter.

Luckily, I could prove my thoughts weren't just the ramblings of a crazed conspiracy theorist. I did the research. Why? Because the ambassadors had been so worried about what I was doing, they had offered me a really good job just to stop. I figured I had to be onto something. This sent me back into my job search with renewed vigor, and I found my new workplace a week later. The Athena Partnership was a small law firm, but it was very, very interested in what I had to say, and I had a lot to say. I shared every bit of information that I had collected with them, and they put me on the case full time. It would have been absolutely perfect if not for that one small obstacle that you always find, just at the cusp of contentment.

Actually, it was less of a small obstacle and more of a giant wall that all working adults constantly have to face. A deadline. Twice each year, all ambassadors gather together to hear the problems that cannot be solved in an election or in a more private setting. The P.U.C.- Planetary Unity Conference.

It was set for two and a half weeks after I was hired, and the company had managed to get a spot for me to state my case. It was a hot topic, still, and lobbyists and some other small companies had discreetly helped out. It wasn't a lot of time, and it wasn't an easy case, and I was not as ready as I had figured I was.

I spent the time I had working as hard as I possibly could. Every waking moment I spent looking either at a screen or around my shoulder for a super spy with a laser gun. Rosa dealt with a lot of the other matters, like reminding me that just because coffee could keep me awake into the wee hours of the morning did not mean that I should let it. She was right, I had been up for 20 hours straight, and what I thought was a brilliant nine hundred words on the morality of discovery had actually turned out to be complete gibberish upon later review.

"Whhen we fonf oirselbes on anoyher planet, that foesnt mean it's ours. The planet has people. It happens to hold, it may houlf a popukatuion, this populatoin of living thingsa (Or rocks, do rocks have rigt s>?_) eeserved their planet. It is nt our planet, we hav a pl ent"

[Nova Bale's P.U.C. Presentation-redacted material]

Still, I was forced to overextend myself, despite the efforts of my roommate and my new coworkers. I even completed my finishing touches to the presentation while on the plane to the conference itself. Was I an old white male, the kind that these eighty-year-olds were used to from the generation before them? No. Was I stressed, sleep deprived, and desperate? Unfortunately. Though, I was also smart, dedicated, and armed with enough energy pills to make a fish fly. So, was I ready? I had to be.

CTR 3

"Overconfidence is the comfort of fools as they walk the path of a mediocre life. It fans the flames of an arrogant kind of complacency, burning ambition stifled underneath. Truly, you need a quiet sort of confidence to embrace that your life can improve, to grow a cautious pride that you won't find destroying you. In this caution, and this kind of careful confidence, dreams are fulfilled."

[Allister Sosedge, Crimes of Confidence]

I didn't have a lot of time to process what was happening after we arrived at the conference. I'd landed later than most, to give myself as much time as I could spare to complete my presentation, which was six hours from when I arrived. The conference check in started one hour after I arrived. The venue changed every year. That year it was London.

Clouds hung heavy overhead, the consistent city weather serving as an odd comfort for me, as I dropped my bags at the hotel I'd be spending the night in. The walk to the convention was short, but it still took a full forty-five minutes before I was able to enter the arena-sized room where the conference was being held. Cruelly nicknamed the Great Solarium, the round building was topped by a large, clear dome that mainly showed skies made dark by hanging groups of clouds. I stared at them as I went through security. One check, two, x-ray, my favorite pen went missing. Then I was through a metal detector, and I had begun staring at the crowds around me. I saw Calix as I was emerging through the final checkpoint, entering the stadium-like space and finding a seat among the crowds staring at the arch of seats along the wall. Each chair waited to be filled by ladies and gentlemen of the highest juries of the world.

They started filling the seats minutes later, beginning with lower ambassadors and ascending to the top seven. Close to the seats of each group sat men and women in suits and formal wear.

Officially titled as advisors, the whispers named them "messengers." They were the ones that made sure that what the ambassadors wanted to happen, happened. Calix sat among them, standing out both for his age and, of course, the giant metal hole in his face. I still couldn't figure out why he left it visible. It made a statement, but skin grafting and prosthetic replacements were so common that it would be no inconvenience to someone of his status to make himself look normal. Handsome even. His eyes silently scanned the room, and I made an attempt to mimic the cool gaze. Hours passed with the steady sound of voices, one presentation following another. My thoughts grew clumsy and my mind clumsier. I sorted through the presentation in my hands, all planned through. As much as I would have enjoyed a passionate speech born from the heat of the moment, that wasn't happening.

The minutes dragged by, achingly slow. Finally, the moment came. My throat was dry, and my heart was racing. This was the most important thing that I had ever done, leaps and bounds above every class presentation or public speech. I wasn't even a prosecutor, I was in research building. The people around, watching, deciding, were impossibly important as well. I honestly never thought I would be in this conference, in the company I was in, standing in front of the people I was standing in front of. That just didn't happen for most people. As I walked up, I was stopped by a man with a tablet and a frown. He checked whatever was on the screen and looked me up and down. "Ms. Bale, our records say you were born in South America. Do you need a translator?" He spoke really, really slowly, and I had to take a moment to control my temper.

Decades before, a law had been passed by the same conference that English was a necessary first language. The tradition had worn off since the Third Wave, but I'd learned it first, and Spanish second. It was infuriating. Instead of blowing up, I just shook my head and moved past him.

When I got up, my voice was shaky, and I spared no time on introductions or civilities.

"My name is An- My name is Nova Bale, and I stand in front of you-" I faced the crowd instead of the ambassadors "-not for any personal gain, but for the benefit of an entire society, an entire world, as well as the salvation of any humanity we may retain. There is a species on the planet Janus that are, at best, being exploited. because of our deeply ingrained arrogance, our terrible, world-ending belief that we hold the divine right to take what we want and to fulfill any desire that creeps into our minds. We may not have undeniable photographic proof, but we, here, have the opportunity to complete the quest that a young adult, barely a man, gave his life to complete. Arthur Keene risked all he had for the chance to save this species, and we truly have no choice but to give up the bare minimum to even pursue this case, to put those who may be guilty at the mercy of these high courts, these lawful judges." I turned back, scanning the carefully emotionless faces of the levels of our government, all seated behind me. Addressing them, I continued, my voice growing louder as I seemed to rise out of my body.

"It is not the nature of Mankind to hold still. We, as a species, are in a constant search for a way to move forward. This is why we are not bashing each other with stones and rocks and are instead joined together in learning. We have created a society that welcomes change, aims for advancement, and embraces the future. In doing this, we have followed the calling we were all born with. We yearn for a challenge, to move our race forward into a brilliant future. This calling has brought us out of war and economic collapse, replacing these horrors with the society you all know and are constantly aiming to improve. However, if we can see what change does for us, how unity brings our society such gifts, why do some cling to painful past ideals?"

Images flashed across my mind. Chauvinists, racists, people who said I was too young to do this; not smart enough or from a good enough background to do that. I let their opposition fade into the back of my mind as I scanned the faces of my audience, the faces of each man and woman, each civilian, each lawyer or businessman or politician picked out from the chaos of the crowd.

"Why, I ask you all, educated people, the golden ones of our nation, why do weak-minded cowards cling to their hatred, their impossible arrogance? They are not simply holding our society still, but are driving us backwards. The noose of our own fear is dragging us away from the advancement of our entire race. How could we hope to improve, to prosper, to expand, if we hold tight to our own false belief of our divine right to our desires? Would we truly let our pride keep everything—our children, our nations, our worlds—from their best selves? Will we let it create a wall between us and the future that that minority, that loud, hateful, too-large minority fears? I say we trust our instinct, our base humanity, and allow our society to shine in the light of a new era. An era of unity truer than any we have yet achieved. Let us shed our hatred, our superiority, and walk into our future, unburdened by these, the true sins of humanity."

I took a half breath, sobering. "I cannot say that freeing this species will accomplish all of this, but it is a start. It's a symbol of goodwill not just for causes of social justice, but for environmental justice and conservation, and to those who reasonably want to protect our world and others from the suffering and mistakes humans have already made. We almost died out. We all know it, even if we refuse to think about it. Our world nearly killed us in retribution for the years and years of poisoning and leeching and all that we made it suffer through. But, we survived, and we, for a short time, had an ideal that we could improve the world. Now, if we claim the duty to explore other planets, we also have to claim the duty to protect them and their inhabitants. We've seen the colony broadcasts. Though there is no proof that they are objective or unedited, they show that the colony was founded for research on the basic fact that the Tril-Chi-rosapiencdae possess human level intelligence, and thus a human-level capacity for love and hate and good and bad. We can't waste this potential, and the potential of other species, discovered and undiscovered, to improve our world and to further strengthen and expand our union. All I request is the ability to safely continue my work, and again be met when I have a more conclusive case, and to let that case be judged in a proper, without-a-shadow-of-a-doubt-official, court of law. Thank you."

My knees had turned to jelly, and my tongue felt as if it filled half of my mouth. The last few sentences had falling out of my lips with what seemed to be barely any pause between the words. There was a flurry of rushed typing as they communicated, the motions rushing up one layer of power at a time. After what felt like forever, one announcer spoke, rising slightly in his seat.

"You may continue your research." The stress began to melt out of my shoulders before the statement was finished. "On Janus, where you can see your subjects up close."

That wasn't part of the plan. I supposed I had to be grateful, but I instead remained in a numb sort of shock for the remainder of the conference. There's nothing to say about the days after that. My night in the hotel was full of restless sleep, as well as the nights until I was scheduled to begin my trip to Janus.

CTR 4

"Shattered words, shattered bones
Broken mirrors, broken homes
Icy husks of green vein
Fingerprints on window panes
A breath of air, beneath my wing
A wanderlust, a need for spring."

[Annaliese Vienkra, Flowers in Snow, A
Retrospective]

ARTHUR

When I fell through the gaping mouth of the mine, traveling through the rapidly closing darkness, it felt like forever. An eternity in silent motion. Yet, you'd be surprised how quickly an eternity can end. The next time I felt the tug of conscious thought, it came with a searing headache and the orange-tinted stabbing of dull light filtering through my eyelids. I wanted to cover my eyes, but it seemed as if it would be too much effort. Opening them seemed like too much effort. Everything seemed like too much effort. Still, I forced them open, my vision blurring the ceiling above me. I blinked, my eyelids heavy and the ache in no way dulling. My view of the dark, jagged, rock above cleared slowly and the luminescent plants clinging to its rough surface moved in and out of focus.

That was a pretty big clue to where I had woken up, but there were still a lot of questions I needed answers to. I didn't think; I just sat up, fast, and my vision went dark again.

The next time I woke up, I went a little slower. I stared straight up until I was ready to stand and remain conscious at the same time. It wasn't easy, but I forced myself to my feet.

As I looked down, I saw my clothes were ripped, hanging off my limbs in ribbons. The yellow tint of fading bruises marred the space between healing cuts. My left side had the worst of it, my shoulder felt loose, and my leg wasn't bending the way it normally did. I sat down again, and pain flared up in my ribs. I glanced at my side, once, and bile rose in my throat. I couldn't look behind me, but I reached back and dragged my fingers over my skin. I won't describe it.

I felt stiff and clumsy, and my ears were ringing. It seemed loud, too loud to be what I remembered of the mines. I lifted my hand to my temple, stifling a cry. When I moved it away, there was no blood. My various injuries had been treated, or cleaned, at least, and bandaged. Temporarily bandaged—there were weeks of fixing myself up after that, but I won't go into detail there either.

I braced myself against the wall and moved forward. As soon as my hand made contact, my senses flooded with the noises of conversation and the ringing began to fade. Exhaling a deep sigh of relief, I scanned the room.

The walls were stone. I felt the rock, and it seemed more carefully cut and chipped than what I remembered of the hallways. The bed was low and hard, and this, I figured, was what had caused my back to ache. That and just about everything else.

The rough cloth hanging off the slab I'd been sleeping on looked as if it were scattered with drops of blood, each red droplet faded from age and care. I dropped to the floor, spotting a pile of dark green plants dumped next to the bed, barely illuminated by the faint glow of the ceiling. I focused on the small details: headache, blood, strange plants, and a million unanswered questions. And each morning for months after that, I opened my eyes to shaking limbs and pain with every movement as the Trillers' best medical cures could do nothing more for me than prevent infection and starvation. I'm not complaining, staying alive was enough. I settled into the community, made myself comfortable in the stark room, and was more content than I ever had been. This was all despite the aches and pains and inherent loneliness of being distinctly different from those that surround you.

To summarize, I didn't die.

Most of the shock wore off a few days after I first woke up, but the pain didn't. It took a few days for me to start walking. I started around my room, then down the hall, twice a day without fail. It hurt. It hurt more than anything has ever hurt. It hurt in my hands, my head, when I breathed and walked and wrote. I splinted my limbs and bandaged what I could and found that the pain in my head eased when my mind was filled with the sounds that echoed through the rock. The hurt didn't go away, but it faded behind other, more important things.

There was no time to sit and sulk and suffer. Every member of the mines did something. Children were forced to work the moment they were able, everyone who couldn't mine tended to the injured or cooked or crafted or farmed. To start, I clawed and smashed at the walls of the mines, chipped with sharp edges and pulled with flat sleds. That hurt too, and I was no good at it. I did it for about four days before it began to take longer and longer for me to recover from each trip.

I'd spent my time in the colony learning; I've said that before. I learned anatomy and biology and problem-solutions that made sense in my head. I'd spent hours bent over surgical holograms and sleepless nights poring over textbooks. I had a really specific degree somewhere, and it put "Dr." before my name. So I started lingering in the medicine rooms, poring over the notes they had. They were vague and spread out and focused more on spirituality than I would like, but I found my niche there.

After I figured out how I could help, I didn't do much else.

By that time, I could make it to the large cavern where they ate and told stories, when they could. I sat away from the clusters that they broke into, my focus on reading and translating. I was mainly left to myself, for about a week of this, not paying attention to the ground plant based meals or the talking or anything beyond the words I studied until my eyes grew blurry from exhaustion.

It was day three of joining them, I think, when someone approached me. Not Ve, Ve only met me in the room I slept in. He was taller, and a little older, and the hair over his forehead was more wiry. He sat by me and placed a bowl at my side. I hadn't eaten that day. I was unsure, but lifted it into my lap at his urging nod. He seemed satisfied with that, and left. The food had taste that night.

Another day passed, and he approached me again, pointing to the fire. It cast warm shadows over his weathered palm, and I moved closer. This pattern continued until I approached his cluster with no hesitation. Ve told me he was a teacher, unable to mine. That next morning, I made my first non-work trip, shaky steps moving barefoot through the stone pathways towards the small section of teaching rooms. My palm was dragging across the wall, and I felt his voice echo through. Then there was a deep rumbling, and I saw a ripple pass through the miners around me. There was dead silence, and then the world burst into shouting.

Children were pouring from the entrance of the hallway, dust was shaking from the ceiling, and the deafening sound of rock cracking echoed off the walls until it was a roaring that filled my brain. I took a step towards the hall before feeling long fingers catch my clothes, dragging me to the shelter of a small nook.

It was silent again a minute later, and then the sounds of mining rang out again. Of course they went back to work, what choice did they have? The tunnels didn't just collapse on their own.

They never managed to dig out the teacher's body.

CTR 5

*"The joy of discovery rarely comes alone,
often followed by unpredictable side effects...
From the bond strengthened with others who
share the joy, to a kind of isolation that
comes from a deeply emotional event that most
will be unable to even imagine, much less
understand...There is something distinctly
tragic in the quiet kind of sacrifice made
only by an explorer's choice to distance
themselves from average society."*

[Niamh Wyan, Tragedy]

NOVA

The days before the journey were odd. Unusual. Anxious. I
knew it was low risk, that space travel was something that

thousands of people, at least, were doing that very moment. But I'd never considered going to a colony. Rosaline had thought about it, to get rid of debts from school, and I'd talked to friends about it, moving to one of the planets with city-dense populations. Janus wasn't one of those, though.

I was riding on a supply ship, as there were no new workers going up to the colony. Rosaline helped me pack— she insisted on it. It was a three week trip that could've been done in half the time, in a newer ship. Since it wasn't classified as a passenger ship, there was no station, just an air lot after a four-hour ride upstate. Rosaline rode with me, and she handed me a bright red lunchbox with a single banana inside.

"No fruit in space."

That made me tear up. I was scared, really. I'd been staying on my normal routine, pretending that things were just as they had been, but they weren't.

My sneakers clanged against the metal of the short stairs as I climbed up into the ship's main entrance, my main bag already inside and the lunchbox held tightly between my hands. Rosa waved, and I waved back, even when I couldn't see her.

The trip was long, achingly so. It stretched out in work and TV and talking to the pilot, whose name was Liam. He had a daughter about my age, and he was Scottish and complained about how people were purposely bringing the accent back. I wouldn't tell him, but he had a slight brogue.

Obviously, it's not the longest interplanetary trip, but after the adrenaline of preparing, it felt so slow. But every day we were moving past new stars and new planets, which we drew closer to. It was the one good thing about the trip, seeing the stars up close. I couldn't even imagine what it was like for Liam, to get to do it all the time.

When we finally landed, I was standing at the window with my bags in hand. I focused on the sandy colors of the surface, with wispy clouds tinted pink even from above by the giant red sun floating close to it. There were faint patches of blue and dusty green covering sections of the world, true nature. Not brown or gray or marred by the work of humans.

My first step upon landing was nothing climactic or extraordinary. It was like an exit from any other vehicle, just a little lighter. I jumped a few times before realizing several men and women were standing at the door of the colony. I didn't notice too much in the colony, the surroundings passing over me in a wave of metallic silver and plastic panes. Unfortunately, most doors were closed; I could even hear some slams as I was guided towards them. The group made no effort to give me any kind of a tour, silently walking down the white and gray tinted hall. Their steps were short, clipped, making soft clicking noises, and they were dressed similarly, with just a few small differences in the uniform of plain jackets closed neatly over any kind of shirt underneath, with small symbols above a name pin on the breast pocket.

I was guided towards a room, which was alone, and seemed thrown into the building plan. I'd only seen suites of three or six when I researched the colony. The interior was white-walled and filled completely with a small desk, dresser, and a plain bed, low to the floor. The floor was partially covered with stacks of boxes and fallen papers, but nothing important. There was a second, broken, chair in the corner. There were posters on the wall, and cracks behind them. There was a rectangular window that I stared at as the door behind me closed with a soft puff of air, hitting the wall with a kind of finality.

The window was near the ceiling, long and narrow, with just the barest view of the courtyard that shared a wall with it. Stiff sheets shifted under me as I lowered myself onto the bed and removed my screen from my bag. I decided there was nothing I had to say, even to my most private record. At least the excitement was back, along with the urge to do good, and the nerves. I was actually going to see an alien species, and that was a big deal for me back then. Would be for most people, except the poachers and their clients, or those in other colonies. Finally, I felt the tingles of excitement travel from my fingertips to my spine, washing over the fear that had settled there before.

It was another restless night, scattered with unsettling dreams that faded like wisps of smoke once I was awoken by my alarm. I had no desire to eat with the colony's crew, instead digging into the package I had brought to the colony from the ship's supplies. I ate a granola bar while curled on the white floor at the foot of the bed.

I sent a few messages back to Earth, because half of my family was convinced that I was dead, and the other half had forgotten I left. After that, there was a loud, insistent knock on the door that brought me immediately to my feet. At the door, I was met by a short woman with a high ponytail and a tall, stern-looking man with a shadow of a beard tracing his jaw. He had to be in his fifties, with a face that I recognized from old news reports. He was a little older, a little less clean shaven, but still identifiable as one of the first settlers of Janus. "It's an honor to meet you Mr. Keene, and my condolences for your lo-." He cut me off then, nodding sharply.

"Everyone is sorry, but it's in the past." I was more than a little unsettled by his cold nonchalance but allowed myself to let that pass. "This is Lyla Caolano" He pointed in the vague direction of the woman "She's a leading cartographer of this planet. She will show you what you wish to see."

The cartographer had a polite smile on her face. "Where can I take you?" she chirped brightly, moving to let me step out as the explorer curtly whispered a message to her. Before I could even wonder what he'd said, the sounds of his footsteps were already fading.

"Everywhere. Most importantly, the mines that are allegedly being used to exploit an entire species of alien." I matched her bright tone and polite smile, keeping my face mask-like. Hers wavered for just a moment as she turned away from me, making her way down the hall, in the direction of the entrance I had used yesterday. I barely remembered to grab my notepad and pen as we rushed down the hall.

Ms. Coalano wouldn't look back at me, and I didn't know why. Maybe she feared my research would make her lose her job. A painful bolt of guilt hit me, but I shook it off. Research jobs should be saved, and if not, the lives of the species had to be placed above my guilt. We left the cooled building and emerged into the sun. I had a few moments to stare at the world around me as my guide went to find a vehicle for us to begin our tour on. I could spot various members of the colony through the plastic panels. I made no effort to speak with them, and they seemed to be making an effort not to talk to me.

At least I could fool myself that it was mutual, and I did, a calm smile on my face as the woman forced to speak with me returned in an old vehicle. It was reminiscent of the last century's golf carts, that have since been replaced by more efficient modes of travel. I was sure I had spotted some more modern carts, but I didn't mention them.

The thoughts, thankfully, were easily lost, scattered away in the mass of excitement building in my chest. I was about to see things that few humans had, to meet an intelligent species, and possibly even help save them. This goal rose above all other thoughts and worries, drowning them out in a hesitant hope, growing stronger. I watched the landscape pass, caught up in my thoughts. My guide seemed to be having her own interesting thoughts, a pensive frown tugging at the corners of her lips. It wasn't my place to ask, and even if it was, I didn't really want to.

I spent my time focusing on a hundred things, so nothing really stayed in my mind for long. When the car slowed, my racing thoughts slowed with it, fading into a background of anxious anticipation. We stepped out together, pacing slowly over to what had at first looked like an expansive shadow spread across the rough ground. I admired the green of a nearby farm, always grounded by the sight of growing plants. I clung to that steadiness as we grew closer to the solid darkness, pausing several feet before its jagged lip.

My hand flew to my mouth in irrepressible shock. My heart seemed to halt in my chest and tears pricked my eyes. The horrors, the impossible inhumanity that could only be caused by humans. Taking in bits of information such as the way the working figures moved and the sounds they made, I was guided down stairs. Stone stairs, immediately bringing a cool draft and the smell of something dark.

The cartographer stopped near the bottom, a couple steps in front of me "Are you sure you want to go down here?"

"Of course,"

"They said…I'm sorry, I need this job!" She turned and shouldered past me.

I stared back at her for a moment, in time to catch her bolting up the half dozen steps. She paused at the top, her mouth opening before she seemed to reconsider and close it. I took a step back before I saw the slamming of a door that looked newly installed. I looked back down, my head clearing. The light at the bottom was cut off by another door scraping shut. I ran down, swearing. I heard the grumbling of a rock unlodging itself from the wall, pulled by the slamming of the door. My comm didn't work, and I had no plan.

Naively, I had figured that this project wasn't corrupt enough to kill someone who tried to stop them. It was ridiculous, an action movie concept that absolutely did not happen to real people. Not yet ready for death, I ran towards the thin strip of light at the bottom, my knees and elbows scraping on the stone as I fell. I lay for a moment, dazed, before I was suddenly somewhere else, out of the cool shadows and under the hot sun again. I opened the eyes I didn't realize I had squeezed shut, the light filtered orange through my eyelids.

I took a shaky breath as shadows of rocks flickered over my face. Unable to rise to my feet, I realized, first, that I was out of the stairwell, being pulled along by the miners. Maybe it was the light gravity, but I was practically skipping over the stone ridges of the floor. They must have pulled the door open; maybe the overfunded team of geniuses up in the colony had forgotten that any creature with thumbs and brains could figure out how to open a door. I had to wonder why they would even want to save me after all humans had done. When we finally paused in our movement, back in the shade of another tunnel, I asked the question swirling through my head, eclipsing all other thoughts. "What?" I asked simply, realizing as I said it that they wouldn't understand me. They babbled in a low, gruff tongue for a minute, hands on the walls. The walls almost shook, but, at the time, I discounted that as a hallucination.

"Arthur!" one exclaimed, turning to look at me expectantly.

"Keene?" I attempted.

My vision swayed as I stood up far too fast. So, they knew the boy that had been killed trying to save them. My response sent the group into another round of clamoring. They hushed themselves abruptly, focusing on me. It was unnerving. A hand was extended towards me, and pulled back with red on the fingertips. I wasn't squeamish, but I nearly felt my eyes roll back, my own fingers shooting up to reach around for the gash. I suddenly found it, a cut across my lip and another on the bridge of my nose.

"Ow," I muttered.

Chattering loudly again, the group led me down stone hallways, a few flaking off as we moved past flickering lights and branching mines. We stepped into one shadowed room, filled with a low block draped with rugged fabric and a stone shelf disappearing into the corner with—I blinked. There was a figure leaning on the shelf, blocking most of the light shining from the room's lamp. His back was to us, but the proportions were human.

Most of the others had dropped back, though shifting movements nudged me through the doorway. I cleared my throat, and he turned around. He was deathly pale. I noticed that first. His features were curious, and very human, though his eyes reflected the light just a little too much. His skin was marked by a mess of pink and white lines in various levels of healing that radiated out from one fading scar on his temple. His clothes were patched with the same fabric as the blankets, as ragged as the hair falling past his ears. It hit me in a burst—it was the man from the broadcast. I'd only seen a flash of a face in harsh light, blurred and obscured, but this had to be him, pale and tired outside of a moment of passion.

Things changed just in that moment.

Reverently, I further approached the figure, reaching out. I'm not sure why, I just assumed he was a hallucination of what I figured the boy must look like. I was about a half foot away when he spoke. I'm not ashamed to admit that I shouted, scrambling back halfway to the door. The man stared back with serious brown eyes, waiting a moment for my panic to wind to an end.

"Hi. Who are you?"

THE CALL TO
BE

CTB 1

"Spectacular. That's the only word for it. The only word for being the only one of your species to have ever seen a whole new world. This world, an incredible gold mine of knowledge and science and power. To live among its occupants, to learn with them, to feel almost as if you are one of them, is a joy and acceptance beyond any I have ever experienced."

[Arthur Keene-Opening; Records of the Mines]

ARTHUR

A few times, I'd wished that there was another person down in the mines. That did not make turning from my work to the sight of an odd woman shouting a half foot from my face any less startling.

It didn't feel polite to interrupt, so I waited until the noise faded into silence again.

"Hi. Who are you?"

"Arthur Keene?!" Her eyes were dark and wide. That was a little bit confusing. Not the eyes, the name.

"You can't be Arthur Keene. I'm Arthur Keene. Who are *you*?" Things didn't get clearer from there.

"From the broadcast!"

I moved over, easing her to a seat to check if she had a head injury. There were a few bruises scattered around her hairline, and a nasty gash across her nose. She didn't seem concussed, though. Although she did continue with the nonsense.

"You're dead."

She seemed a little upset that I wasn't. It wasn't a question, when she said it, and her tone made her seem offended at my state of being alive.

"Am I dead??"

She seemed serious. A little concerned, I knelt in front of her and took the opportunity to check her eyes for dilation.

"Not unless I am, and I don't believe in life after death, so I can't be." She showed no symptoms of a concussion, but I was still concerned. "I'm Nova. Nova Bale."

Nova stood, and she stared at me again. It was a good, solid answer. I remember thinking that the name suited her. She was almost brimming with possible energy, a star waiting to shine, to explode, perhaps. Maybe not waiting, in fact. Nova seemed rather eager to move again, rising quickly from the bed and beginning to mutter as she paced the room.

I was prepared to guide her back down, but then I processed her words and was knocked back. Months had passed since I'd woken up that first time, or that second. "I came here to finish your fight." She moved towards me, a calming lilt in her voice and her arms offered out to me. When I shifted away, though, she lowered them and turned her focus from me to the wall. I don't know if she noticed, but her fingers twisted a ring between them.

"Slow down." I plucked the words out from the mess swarming around my brain. This time, I was the one who had to drop down, landing on the bed. My knee clicked. "You mean to tell me that people actually saw that? You're saying that even though it aired on a Union channel, they didn't shut it down?"

This, in the moment, seemed an improbable, if not impossible, thought. I may not have been living on Earth, but I knew about corruption. A world of blackmail, threats, and bribes hidden under a gilded shell. Sounds dramatic, but I've seen it up close, since then, and the shell is very, very thin.

Nova stopped her muttering and looked at me, a frustratingly pleased smile pulling up the corner of her lips.

"They did, but by then, other channels had picked up the signal. They couldn't send threats fast enough. Sure, they tried to discredit you, but they couldn't make people unsee it."

I found myself impossibly thrilled; I had never expected so much. Still, I put the joy on hold, listening intently as she continued.

"You got semi-famous, but-" she paused, pressing her palms together "-not in the way you seemed to be aiming for. You have some fans, people wrote poems and stories about you..." She grinned wryly. "You're the star of these amazingly terrible short films, at least three."

"So people are working for the cause?"

"Well, no. Listen, I think you're amazing. Really amazing. Just, like, awesome" I saw her fingers flutter, her nails clicking together. "But what happened to you was considered, well...a tragedy. Not a wake up call."

Her mouth snapped closed, her eyes showing regret "It's not that people didn't believe you, they just didn't focus on that part...I saw it"

The missed point of it all was a little bit concerning. It wasn't like I'd been subtle about it. Speaking as a member of the race, humans are wildly oblivious and willing to ignore the deeper truths around them. But Nova, she understood what I wanted to say. She had left a safe, normal planet to come and risk her life for what I'd said. She could have *died*—the Union was ruthless!

Though my father could not be described as the epitome of a civil man, my mother was a woman of grace and civility. I had learned as a child that a gift should not be accepted with nothing in return. Following my languages, she had just then given me the greatest gift I had ever received. *Have* ever received. In the moment, though, I had nothing and no way of repaying her for all of the help she seemed willing to give me.

However, she *had* come to free a species she knew nothing about, and that I could remedy. I still believe that no one should have to live in ignorance, especially ignorance of the true nature of their ideals. That's what had led to the environmental failure that had plagued the planet.

Along the topic of being oblivious, I had again let my thoughts and the noise of conversation flowing into my mind drift over her voice. She was still talking, her eyes bright and her hands moving in a continual series of gestures. It was an effort to focus myself, as if I had to find the right frequency to again comprehend her words.

"My ship is only a few days off, we can be back to Earth within the month." She seemed ecstatic, which is why I faltered in my reply, hating to disappoint her so soon, but feeling as if it could be unavoidable.

"I can't go." My face flushed in shame. "I can't even go above the surface. There's no life for me there, especially now that I know there's a movement. It doesn't need me, it has you to lead it!"

I meant every word I said, pushing as much genuine hope into each syllable as I could. That hope, she had given it to me, and I wanted to return it with my own sincerity. I had known her hardly a half hour, I believe, and yet she already seemed light years ahead of me. I was convinced that she alone could provide far more aid to the beings that I had grown to love than I ever could. As much as it pains me still to admit, my meager talents could find few uses in the ranks of human society.

Somewhere deep in my mind, I knew those thoughts were the result of what I had been told, directly, or through offhand comments or actions. That didn't mean they were wrong. I had once idolized the man who made those comments, and that worship couldn't have been born from nothing.

I considered all this in that moment as her face fell, weighted with disappointment. Her hands halted their movements too. Though the idea that I was basically useless may have been what I had been taught, it happened to also be what I believed.

"It's not a movement, Arthur, it's a ripple, and the waves outwards are weakening. You could change that."

That hope, I love it now, but at the time, it seemed she had placed her faith in me *far* too quickly. I knew she was looking for some martyr who sacrificed himself, who poetically gave the greatest and final measure of his devotion to his cause. When I looked at myself, though, I saw someone who never had anything to give, and who had broken himself in a final, futile push to be exceptional. It was hard for me to share the truth with her: I knew I had no great destiny. In fact, I had quite literally been pushed into the extreme.

I prepared myself to share the unfortunate news, but her words brought me pause.

"You know that these creatures aren't savages. They saved your life, and mine."

I saw her turn her head, glancing around for them. I spent much of my time with them, but they often left me when I was sleeping, and they seemed to have cleared out right then.

"Arthur, listen. We have the chance to return the favor. They don't deserve a life of fear and oppression. Few are as prepared as you are to face the tyranny on my planet—our planet—and start the path to ending the tyranny here."

"Your planet," I corrected. She may have had false beliefs about what kind of hero I had made myself, but she knew no measure large enough to capture the devotion I had for Janus at that time. Or, maybe she did know, because she already found herself sharing it, in some small way. Maybe she'd just wanted to make me feel guilty, if she happened to be that kind of person.

I assumed she wasn't, as I sort of already trusted her, but it's always safer to remain wary. No matter the reason, she didn't understand that her words did nothing but enforce my need to remain in this place. I couldn't tell her why. There were no words that fit, and certainly not in any human tongue.

If nothing else, I decided that I could show the extraordinarily passionate woman the world I'd been living in. I knew from the horrors that they endured to the small scraps of beauty. The pride. The unbreakable spirit.

Silently, I walked out of the room and into the tunnel. Nova hesitated before she hurried after. My bare feet hardly registered the points of rocks beneath my step, only feeling the unity and the connection passed through my skin. I still felt clumsy next to the grace of the Trillers. Standing at the edge of the tunnel system, I waited until Nova completed her approach, gesturing into the almost darkness.

"Are you ready to see what you're fighting for?"

CTB 2

"The human instinct to pack-bond is one of the species' most miraculous features. It has led to many deaths, particularly the deaths of those who mistakenly believed that predators shared their instincts to unite. However, this instinct has also brought wild success to our species…a human can find joy in the company of any "being" from a rock with a face on it to a manually controlled bot to a dog, a wolf, or a lion. This, in theory, could make us one of the galaxy's finest diplomatic species, or one of the worst."

[Li-Riem Vran, The Earthly Pack]

NOVA

The tunnels were long, and they sloped off into the darkness ahead. Fires flickered every ten feet, throwing small, faded circles of brightness across the stone. The stone itself was dotted gray and red, brown and black. It was rough, large-grained, and the walls were patterned with a natural ruggedness.

With large pieces taken out of the walls in a seemingly random pattern, odd, alien shadows were cast onto the debris scattered floor. The irregular noise of my steps faltering over the small stones added to the overall melody of workers as they chipped away in huge caverns. I could just barely see them as I followed the fleet-footed male in front of me, justifiably on edge.

Arthur could manage the path as well as any of the native miners that we passed, his shoeless feet maneuvering around hollows and small uplifts in the ground. Still, despite this agility, his fingers remained planted firmly on the tunnel wall, one side or the other. His skin practically glowed in the dim light, made paper pale by lack of sunlight. His hair, too, was a dull brown. But his eyes—when he looked back at me I saw them shine beyond the odd way they caught the light. I was fascinated each time he spun to face me, a soft smile almost erasing all the pink and white gashes that webbed across his skin, and dark irises that shone with the mind of a man always thinking, always calculating and analyzing.

They also showed a man content, a man at peace. The smile faded as we came across a pile of randomly stacked rocks, an nonconformity on the rough flatness of the walls. There was just one stone whose placement seemed intentional, flat and carved painstakingly with alien symbols.

He ran his hands over those carvings, lips moving in silent prayer. It seemed right to leave him alone, but a group of miners were approaching and so I found myself forced into a position at his side—a position I've held since. I asked nothing, but he answered.

"Humans don't usually come down here." He seemed to remove himself from that group. "They're fine with staying clean on the surface, unless the miners' load is light. They monitor them closely, especially the upper levels. The Trillers are forced to live where they are told, to work where they are forced. They can barely teach their children. They can barely pray or learn or love."

He seemed boiling over with silent fury, his teeth gritted and jaw set decisively. I had nothing to say. There were no words.

He continued. "They tried to set up a school for some of the older children, tried to teach them their culture, to pass on their heritage. Somehow, someone on the surface found out. They collapsed the whole section."

His hands were shaking, one pushed against the wall and the other pressed lightly against the carved stone. "The children, they survived, but one teacher was caught. He was buried by rubble. I saw it…His body was left under there. They don't even live them the right to bury their dead, not even giving them the dignity…." His voice trailed off as he pulled his hand away from the carving.

"What does it say?"

Arthur looked at me seriously, gnawing on his lip. He spoke a name, softly, one that I could not repeat even if I tried. Then, simply, "'Hero, Teacher, Father, Friend. May you live on in our hearts, and our stars and shadows.'" I was silent, allowing the simple epitaph to fill the space around us, like a bubble.

Until it popped, and the silence became deafening.

I waited for him to speak first. It was his right, at least, to decide when we would continue our walk and our conversation. He started walking before he spoke again, letting the silence pass. "I'm sorry, but the world isn't just a concept to back for a fight or social revolution. It's full of actual pain, of suffering."

What world isn't?

I thought out loud as we continued our walk. "Do they always collapse the tunnels? That just seems a little inefficient. Not that it's not also cruel, but thinking from their perspective—"

He stiffened, a small frown forming on his face. "No.. They usually don't put in that kind of effort. They'll send a spray of debris or maybe bullets, if they're really mad. You can hear them while they do it, comparing hits. Sometimes they come down, rough up some random miners."

Mentally, I looked back on the people we'd passed.

They wore defeated looks on their faces and their feet dragged with each step. But some were worse than simply hopeless. They had bruises and scrapes marking their faces and limbs. Some had limps or dragging legs, an arm that hung loosely or was held in a way as to not move too much. It was hard to watch, but, of course, it must have been harder to live through. Feeling ashamed of myself, I shook off the thoughts as Arthur continued.

"Sometimes they fire down a few shots. It's been happening more often." He paused to greet each group we passed as we made our way into a more populated area. I couldn't help but silently admire the way the Trillers moved. I took a breath and listened to the way they sent their voices echoing around us. It was quietly mesmerizing, and I was drawn into the secret world. I slowed as Arthur guided us neatly through a cavernous mine. His own limp was suddenly more obvious, now that I was focusing. I stared until I couldn't bear to focus on his pain anymore. The ceiling hung jagged above us, and I stared up at it as he spoke.

"I just wish I could help more." The young man's eyes trailed over the masses of workers, their dark figures moving to an irregular beat. His hands had curled into fists, and as I stared down the hall, I saw just how right he was about the pain in the world.

Then, I noticed something else. His fingernails were scraped down to stubs, surrounded by shallow scratches. His fingers were as bloody and calloused as if he had tried to join the miners in their work.

As Arthur drew ahead, back into the tunnels, I felt the sharp prick of tears at the corners of my eyes. How could I take him away from this? Who would be cold enough to pull him from what made him care in a way that I had never seen in the people of Earth? He was free of the plague of apathy that infected so many, stripping them of their empathy, stealing their passion and dragging out every care in their life. This cause had restored that passion and that care in him, multiplying it tenfold. He held the strength of suffragists, the boldness of marchers waving their banners at pride parades, and the simple craving for a better world seen in old pictures of teenage environmental activists. Maybe if there had been more like him, our own world wouldn't have fallen apart. This life, this place, these people—they did that to him. Who could be so cruel as to separate him from that?

These thoughts were further solidified in my mind as I heard a hesitant pride creep into his voice, bordering dangerously on happiness. "I've helped in all ways that I could." We had entered a more properly lit room, halting at the doorway.

Trillers, bruised and bloody, their limbs askew. Their faces were pale and sickly, dark rings coloring the space under their eyes.

"I can help them," he said seriously, making an eager gesture towards a shelf of scrolls on the wall. He was rambling about their anatomy but none of the words registered in my mind. He had already left by the time I looked up from the bodies on the floor, though I caught the last flash of his form as he slid out the door, a small pile of the basic scrolls and hand-bound books held carefully in his arms and earnest apologies spilling from his lips.

Not having the same level of professional intent that he did, I found myself again trailing behind like a lost child. I hadn't been without purpose in months, hadn't been as lost as I then seemed to be, as alone as one could feel while standing in a hidden world that literally echoed with the noises of life.

The air hung heavy with the burdens of hundreds of beings, the pain settling into my lungs. My shoulders bent under the weight of a tribe's sorrows, though I suddenly felt another, more selfish pain. I wasn't invited or born into this

113

world, but I was welcomed by these people, by Arthur. They offered me some place within them.

They had saved my life, and I had done nothing of any consequence for them. All the politics and speeches and training in law school couldn't help them that moment. That was the only thought I could make clear in my mind as I again focused on my surroundings. I had come upon a rough doorway, the room half visible and shining as a portal of light in its surrounding of gray flatness.

I paused at the entrance, the beings inside caught in a private moment that I had no right to intrude upon. There was only one adult in the room, and the rest seemed to be children-smaller and less lean than the adults, though still plagued with the signs of malnutrition. These children were forced to grow up in a world where it was clear to them that they were seen as living tools, that they were destined for a life of pain and forced labor.

But they were young. They held that spark of youth that changes worlds and shapes history. The teacher spoke bravely, though she held a defeated look in her eyes as she struggled to share with these children the inventions of their past. I couldn't believe that the school was still running, with all that Arthur had described. A rough roll of paper was held in her hands, its surface covered in dark brown symbols that were crammed into each corner in a pattern vaguely reminiscent of lines of Sanskrit. My school poor, but nothing like this. Our classes had been large, but we weren't crowded in groups of ten or twelve, kneeling on stone to study from a single piece of worn paper. Still, we hadn't held the same hope they did. We weren't being left the same lives they were. We were inheriting a broken world, but their world was meant to break them.

The moment I saw those children, so determined to live, to make gold out of the granite that their lives were carved from, my heart tore itself in half. If my camera had worked, I may have taken a thousand pictures. Not to slap on a billboard, or to broadcast around the world, but to remind me of why I would fight this battle no matter how many obstacles fell into my path. It seems foolish now, that I once believed these images could leave my mind, especially the face of one feminine child whose dark eyes burned with a flame that told anyone who saw that she would not be satisfied with the life she lived then.

She was the first to notice me, calling out a few clear words that excited the class into a whirlwind of small children swirling around my legs and shouting questions in their language. I hadn't exactly had the time to read over the translations that were stacked about the room I'd found Arthur in earlier.

I wanted to, more than I could have guessed. The language was widely ranged and fascinatingly intricate in its pronunciation. They all drifted back a few feet when the teacher spoke, stern. The child I had focused on before was the last to allow her voice to fade out, her gaze set on me, along with many other sets of large, dark eyes. Members of the species, as a whole, were smaller then humans of the same age and gender. To see so much intelligence in the gazes of figures so small was startling. The teacher moved through the ranks of her charges and stared up at me for a moment, her approach allowing me to really note the grace of the movement. She hesitated for an uncomfortably long second, silence again lingering heavy in the air. She seemed to be forming her lips around a word she wasn't used to, and I knew what that was like, so I waited.

"Teach." She gestured around, the words sounding low and archaic as they burst from her lips. They'd learned a few words from Arthur as he had learned their language.

I nodded seriously, gesturing vaguely to myself and enunciating, "Help Arthur." They all nodded excitedly, the teacher's sorrows lifting from her face for a moment. I wanted to help more, so I spoke my name next, "Nova. Bale."

Though they seemed no less joyful, there was a mildly stunned moment of silence before the children all launched into introductions. Their names were short and varied, a handful of letters practically pronounced as a sentence. The child I had noticed above others joyfully crowed "khe-hvvichar" a name I now know to be spelled Kvir. Their pasts had been erased, their history and culture twisted and torn away from them. Yet, the children prospered. They became, or remained, a society that was giving and humane and welcoming above that of much more advanced civilizations. I had to help, and my place in this battle was back on Earth.

To stay would be selfish, as would asking Arthur to leave with me. His fight was there, because he could help them there. I prepared myself to share this realization with him as the teacher called a guide, and I followed him into a different, plain room. It looked similar to the one I had found Arthur in, and I found myself wondering how they had so many rooms free. It felt like I'd first found him a week before, at least, but it'd barely been an hour. Giving myself a chance to think through the events of the day, I dropped onto the slab. My fingers twisted thoughtfully into the fabric, and I could feel its neat weave and its imperfections.

I scarcely moved until Arthur appeared at the doorway, a look of concern on his face. He approached the bed with quick, light steps—used to the low gravity, of course. He paused by the bed for a moment, this man, this genius and this inspirer of a movement looking incredibly uncomfortable until I gave a small nod and he sat down, his long legs folded awkwardly under him.

He had on a colony jacket, I realized, maybe again. I could hardly remember. The small, round buttons marched in a neat line down one side of the coat. Though they had once been proudly embossed with the union's exploration symbol, each mark had since been scratched out and replaced with small, painstakingly carved symbols. Letters in the alien alphabet, I guessed.

"A-Ach-Are you okay?" His voice caught halfway through the sentence, forcing him to end it amid a coughing fit. He remained with one hand pressed to the stone of the wall, and I made a mental note to ask him about that in a less intimate moment.

I nodded faintly, gesturing generally around us. It had been a *long* day. Seeing the way his worried face twitched into a small smile, and taking comfort in it, I prepared to tell him that he shouldn't join me back on Earth. But, again, I had hardly parted my lips to force the words out when he spoke, the thought tumbling out of his brain and spilling off his tongue.

"I'm coming back to Earth."

CTB 3

"To be left behind is one of the great sorrows of mortal life
A world dragged away from under one's feet
By one who leaves, whether leaving behind paradise
Or leaving one to suffer the flames of torture's heat
Our minds, full of stories of loss and woe
We hardly stop to consider the toll on those who leave
No matter how far a man is forced to go
You never seem to consider what cause he has to grieve."

[K. Morles, Sorrow-A Collection of Mortal Poetry]

It wasn't quite the dramatic declaration that Nova insists it was. She didn't see the ten minutes of pacing in the hall, nor the rest of the thought process behind the choice. The moment was also destroyed as I realized that she had been about to speak, and practically fell over myself in apologies for interrupting her.

Though it was mainly me making a fool of myself, I found myself pleased that whatever I did brought a twitch of a smile to her face. A momentary flash of relief from the stress she'd put herself through, all because she saw a glimpse of a video. Because she heard the desperate words of a panicked boy—man, if you choose to be generous. She saw someone with no plan, no idea that he could even have a future, and she saw his prayer, she saw that he was pleading for someone who knew what to do. And she did something. She could have stayed in her home, comfortable and safe. She must have had some sort of life back on Earth. A life she uprooted for the glimmer of hope.

What kind of person would I be if I couldn't leave a home I'd only known for a few months, on a plan that was more than just hope? After the declaration and round of panicked apologies that followed, we sat, silently, for no less than thirty seconds. Then, shockingly, she broke down, hand over her mouth and her shoulders shaking with the force of emotion flowing through her. I was terrified, my hand raising to touch her arm, to comfort her. Until, it slowly dawned on me. She was laughing.

I have no clue what I would have done if she was crying, but the bright, joyful laughter threw me off more than anything else could have. I was left staring silently as the final giggles began to fade, leaving a relieved smile on her face. Then, Nova hugged me. The last time I'd been hugged, it hadn't exactly been something I remember fondly, nor was it a gesture of affection by someone I think of in a fond way. I'm still ashamed to admit that I immediately pulled away from the contact, flinging myself back to the edge of the bed before I realized what I was doing. I consciously halted my retreat. Of course, it was then her turn for unnecessary and panicked apologies. Thankfully, we didn't make silence a pattern. The apology instead dissolved into more hesitant laughter and a sense of guarded optimism that grew in confidence as we spoke and smiled and planned. And there was a high five, which I liked quite a bit.

In the span of maybe twenty minutes, I already knew I would put my life in the hands of this young woman, and I felt confident that she would do the same. Which was, on her part, a terrible choice, but that's neither here nor there. Some time in the rush of thoughts and ideas, Nova mentioned we would have to wait for a little less than a week before we left. The ship she had taken would be forced to move ahead a couple of ports before it could turn back, and it was already a few days' travel away. It was such a short time, certainly not enough for me to say goodbye to the only true home I'd known. At the same time, I had mentally prepared myself to leave that very night, so six days seemed like an agonizingly long time to keep my nerve.

I left her room with my hand pressed against the wall to drown out the ringing in my ears with a thousand conversations. What I really needed was a problem I could solve, a distraction. A hundred issues came to mind. For example, we needed to keep up with Triller news, and it wouldn't exactly be broadcast by the colony. But Nova had a spare working communicator with her that we could leave behind. And then that problem was dealt with and I moved on.

That eased the pain of goodbye, but not enough that I didn't stifle waves of emotion as I continued my actual preparations for leaving. I began to think again, grasping at the tails of a hundred thoughts, at least until I suddenly realized that most of those in the mines would be fading to sleep by now, and it was time I allowed myself, or forced myself, to rest. Distracted, I didn't keep a hand on the now comfortingly rough surface as I entered my room and sat on the bed.

I was struck suddenly with the blasting noise of ringing in my ears. I had mainly enjoyed silence, back in the colony, but the noise of the nearby mines was a constant background, whether I realized it or not. Since the fall, however, silence had become unbearable. The moments that I did not fill with the conversations of many others became painfully sharp needles, an anvil pounding my mind flat. I remember that particular bout. It had been worse than many before it, only outmatched by the earliest rounds. I fell flat against the bed, my vision of the ceiling flickering in and out of blackness. As my stomach rose into my throat, I forced myself again to move, my shoulder slamming into the rough floor as my mind again joined the communal thoughts of others, and the ringing faded into the background, leaving me panting, tears of frustration stabbing at the backs of my eyes.

I wasn't the same man I had been before I fell. I was a man with a purpose. A man who knew his worth. A man with some idea that he might have a future, not to mention what that future might be. But, it wasn't all that heroic and bright. I was a shattered man. A man who couldn't walk right. A man who was forced to let his arm hang loosely at his side so it didn't ache. Who's once surgically-precise hands shook when he wrote. A man with such a sharp mind that he followed close behind Earth's exploring scientists, who had once thrived in isolation. I found myself then to be a man who was fully incapacitated by silence. However, I could speak a language no human had ever bothered to learn, and live in a world full of newness and genuine community viewed by one species as nothing more than a prize to be won through the labor and pain of others thought to be lesser. And fire would be raining from the violet sky before I allowed my father to change my goals; in that respect I had surely become a different man. Never again. Never again would any action of his limit me, because I could think. I could think, I could think. I passed out on the floor, thinking.

That next morning, I will admit, found itself less full of dramatic realizations and life-changing vows against my past. Sure, I was a thinker, but who doesn't love a good menial task? I had a lot of records to finish before I left the mines, and I needed a lot of paper. Unfortunately, the species' close community and lighting-fast communication had not prompted a need for any breakthroughs in printing or writing technology.

They made paper by hand, similarly to how they made their fabric. Personally, I adored watching the process, but I had no time for that today. A makeshift bag full of half-finished documents bounced against my back as I hurried through the halls. All of the few remaining cultural rooms were laid out on low floors, to keep them safe from supervisors too lazy to go that deep in.

The records, libraries and workshops were safely nestled under several hundred feet of rock and caves. I loved the workshops. It was peaceful there, relatively. One bit of culture preserved, safe as it could be from the abuse raining down on the species. Unfortunately, even that remaining piece of culture had been corrupted by human greed.

When once it had been artists working together in the sun of the planet's surface, it was now a half dozen workers and their frantic attempt to keep their people clothed. It was a downhill battle, the once bright colors and patterns lost to the necessity of quick production. Bandages, replacements for clothes ruined in avalanches or attacks, papers to preserve the last vestiges of their fading society. Art was the last luxury they had clung to, but they had been forced to give up even that.

It shouldn't have been a luxury. Culture and history can't just be things oppressors choose to take away. Not that I wasn't extraordinarily proud of this species I had found myself defending, each of them trudging forward stubbornly despite the seemingly unendurable levels of oppression they were forced to live through. Survival, culture, and the attempts to make a life just a bit more bearable were not gifts. They were not options to be taken away by any power.

New waves of disgust at the actions of the people I was born to ran through me as I traveled on my daily tasks through the mines. Through the schools. Through the medical centers and the scraped together homes of the people. Since my conversation with Nova, I'd felt the force of real anger burning in my chest. Perhaps, before our conversation, I had never really believed I could do anything for them. Though I worked with every fiber of my being to ease their burdens just an ounce, that was all I could do. I was trapped in the confines of so poor a life that I could make no difference. Like those on Earth, trudging through days stifled by corruption and the chains of an oligarchy, I did what I could, but could not force myself to hope that it would be enough. But, with this wildly passionate and justice-pursuing addition to my crusade, there was a suddenly and distinctly hopeful new thought in my mind.

Maybe we could do something to change the futures of this planet's occupants.

I'd wanted to, that's not in question. And I had never once considered resigning myself to any notion that I couldn't. But now, this was actual concrete hope.

The artisans had once spread out across the wide expanses of the planet's dry grass and the spreading branches of its trees. In the sun, they thinned and pounded and dried sheets of light wood. The fabric was light, strong, artfully decorated and formed into elegant patterns. I had seen pictures, heard stories. Now, it was a half dozen men and women too old to work, slaving away with rocks and sticks just to keep their family and friends clothed. There was hardly any time to make paper. Wide, round pieces were made almost the same way as the fabric. Thankfully, that day, I had left some papers behind, and I wasn't forced to go off my path in the process of forming my final records. I greeted the workers with the solemnest of greetings, thanked them.

Then I hurried off amid gestures of hope and my promises to return before my final exit. I hadn't told them of my plans to leave, but news travels fast in a colony where people can project their voices fifty meters through stone. Next, I raced through the halls to make my way back to the medical wing where I'd taken Nova the day before. That was where I had found my way of helping the people of the colony, healing them as best I could. I had made detailed records of their anatomy and various medical solutions that I adapted from my work at the colony. Though they didn't know much, they were incredibly lucid and had a clear view of both their own medical problems and those of others. It was as if each colony was a single wolf in a pack that lived stretched out across all surfaces of the planet.

I had to copy my notes and my records, in case there was some kind of attack on the medical center. I would not allow the information of the species to be erased like so much of their culture, nor would I ever be so arrogant as to trust my mind exclusively to store this precious knowledge. I was stressed, and struggling more. Such was the transition from sheltered isolation. From the medical center I retrieved my notes, muttering condolences and reassurances to those patients splayed on the low cots, as well as any advice I could offer to those currently struggling to heal their friends and family. I left the room but didn't go far, turning into a cleared outside tunnel and sitting silently on the rough floor.

Sitting in odd positions or perching on stone for long periods of time was no bother to me. I had a general dull ache pounding in the background of my body, so what difference would a little stiffness make? I spent the rest of that day diligently copying my notes and diagrams. A shock of sadness struck me at each trembling word, my fingers tightening on the pen in my hand. My hands, not as steady as they used to be, disheartened me. The shaking letters, those that were so neat and clear in my mind, sent thoughts of uselessness and doubt flooding my brain. But, my problems faded in the shadow of my cause, and so they were pushed into the back of my mind, where they were left to scrape away at a wound that only grew deeper with each mistake.

I found just a small reprieve from the worries of worthlessness that held a steady post at the edges of my thoughts. Though my hands were not as surgically precise as they may once have been, they could stitch a wound, set a bone back to its proper place, heal all but their own ailments. It didn't hurt that the Chirosapiencidae species, as a whole, were incredibly efficient, for lack of any better word. Their ribs curved, small ridges poking through their shoulder and waist, their torsos thin and caved but for a human-like center, where their major organ systems resided. Their entire pancreatic system was contained in the light, porous material of their spine, their heart and lungs more efficient than any human's, and their bodies containing an internal balance that stored extra water, shifting it from side to side with any weight imbalance and making them unbelievably skilled climbers. Arms were set low and quadruple jointed, stretching out farther than the legs pasted low to their hips.

They were light, with quick heartbeats and quick metabolisms, the entire species lean and strong. Their brains were not yet mapped by me, but I had a sheath of observations about their psychology that I felt no need to copy, keeping it in the personal records that I only consulted in the privacy of my own room. These were the records I found myself consulting after I had spent my day on copies, a night of study awaiting me.

The species moved slowly, deliberately, like a man who was in no rush and wanted the world to share in his languid moments. Though they trudged and hauled heavy stone, their grace was unmatched on any planet I'd seen in the colony's VR. They grew much as they moved, with great grace, and on a deliberate timeline. Infants from birth to about five years, relative to human development, and then from five to about nineteen, they grew faster than humans. Their minds developed exponentially, and they shot up like weeds before fading into a steady pattern for the rest of their lives. Past twenty or twenty-five was when mating started. Careers had been chosen and they were set in their life either in their own colony of birth, or another, and mates were found among their peers that they stayed with until death. There was a very basic economy, jobs assigned from apprenticeships and aptitude in school subjects. A hierarchy was only decided by decision making power, who command fell to in any crisis. The society was neither matriarchal or patriarchal, reproduction occurring externally. Though, I had not found the courage to ask exactly how the mating or birthing process went through its cycle. All else I did know was that it did not affect the pecking order of the tribes. All these facts were included in my notes, along with hundreds of other bits of information I had collected for myself, from observation or found in the records of the people during my months of living in their world.

Most of the rest of my week was packing what few items I could claim ownership of and giving my goodbyes to the mines and its people, as well as promises to return and to continue my fight to free them.

I never break promises.

CTB 4

"Acceptance in any form is a gift beyond any possible assigned value. To be welcomed anywhere is rare, and to be viewed, judged, and still welcomed wholly is one of the rarest events in a human life. Not just to fit and mold yourself into a perfect model of what will gain you acceptance, but to achieve true unity, that is a treasure beyond compare."

[Rellan Phina, The Walls We Hold Between Us]

NOVA

My stay in the mines was a life-altering experience. I had known I was fighting for freedom and to halt the corruption that enslaved a whole tribe of aliens, and to pause the colonization and pollution, but I hadn't truly known the extent of what I was fighting for. I hadn't known I was fighting for families. I hadn't guessed I was fighting for children, like the girl in the classroom. Or for peace and safety and the future of a planet being rapidly colonized and industrialized out of human greed. I felt Arthur's shame in our species, and I found my head bowed much of the time as if under that weight too. But there was no point in guilt. The culture of the beings, the Chirosapiencidae, was astonishing. We, as humans, have lost so much of our culture to war and division and focusing on advancing ourselves right into our own demise. They, however, were united and cultured and civilized, or they had been before we left our dirty hand prints all over their lives.

I didn't have a lot to do during my visit, obviously. There was some work, as there usually is, but not quite enough. I helped some with sorting stone from ore, but I wasn't as skilled as they were. Still, the ones working there, the gray and dusty women, pointed out how to fix my mistakes, gently.

Their art was bright and detailed, from paintings to carvings to the way they wrote with curved lines holding together the words of the sentence. The finest artwork, in my mind, will always be their great patterns of bioluminescent moss, stretched out on the high walls of their most sacred rooms. I only viewed its beauty once, and it is a sight I won't ever fully clear from my memory. I saw the art at what was called, by the species, a naming ceremony.

I found these naming ceremonies another fascinating aspect of the Triller culture, and I diligently recorded each aspect of its history, explained as best as Arthur's friend could in his little English. At birth, a Triller child is only given part of his or her true name, which was already chosen by their parents. They live by this name until they reach a certain level of their maturity, or until their birth tree reaches a certain stage of growth. Birth trees are planted on the day of the child's birth and come from a species of plant that happens to grow in about the same stages as the species. Along with some use of the sun, it's how they measure age. When the tree reaches a predetermined height, the friends and family of the child are drawn together into a private ceremony, and the child is given their true name. To share your true name with any person is a sign of great trust. Really makes one consider how casually we throw our names around. Not me, I haven't used my proper name since high school, but most.

The ceremony I saw was Arthur's, which took place the day before we left the planet. Liam was near, and we were almost prepared to go. I had helped some of Arthur's friends, as many as the workers could spare, to set up his celebration, though I wasn't much use. I mainly watched. I saw how much they truly loved the man who would give up this life for theirs. Not that I, myself, wouldn't do the same by that point. It took nothing past seeing the look of fierce determination in Kvir's eyes to make me fall in love with the species, and make me willing to risk anything to save them.

Arthur, of course, felt the same way. It was easy as anything to tell he did. He worked through each day I spent leisurely exploring the mines, and most of the nights as well. None of my devices worked in the lower caverns, so I could take no photos or videos of the workers, and I had to almost climb up to the guard towers just to send my messages to the ship. But, I recorded all I saw and did, and I had the records written in the neat, if shaky hand of my new personal hero to supplement my research.

I went to law school, but I have never seen a man or woman so devoted to any cause but their own self-serving desires. Arthur would put each member of each council to shame with his passion, and he certainly put me to shame. If he saw a problem, he fixed it. From math problems to a bone fracture to the small engineering issues I had noticed he scribbled in the margins of his notes, he saw no other solution but to fix the problem. We hadn't had much time to connect personally, yet I cared for him as much as any of my siblings, blood or adopted.

That's another reason why I will never forget his naming ceremony. He didn't know it was happening, still babbling about the packing he had to do, which he had done, and the thousands of problems he was making up to solve before he left as Ve and I guided, or dragged, him out of his room and to the doorway of the sacred cavern. He grew quiet as we reached the entrance. As many people as could afford to take a short while to watch the ceremony sat silently in the room, and the rest of the mines seemed to hold its breath.

The darkness swelled joyfully in our pause, slithering around us and resting on my shoulders like a blanket as Ve and I pushed into the faintly glowing room. The audience was a sea of faces, all blurred in the darkness, all united in a force of deep love and respect. They stood as Arthur passed, the tears in his eyes glowing gold in the fading light of torches that were extinguished in front of him. We released our grip on his forearms, though they seemed to be the only thing holding him upright, and faded into the crowd. Just at that moment, I remember, the last torch was extinguished and the room went dark.

Quickly, my eyes adjusted, and I realized I had never and would never see true beauty on Earth. The walls and ceiling had been adorned in a labor of love, jagged surfaces concealed under shifting shapes formed painstakingly out of bioluminescent moss and lichen, shifting gently in the light drafts found under the surface. This gave the whole room a fantastic feeling of movement. I held my breath. At the front of the room was a large, dark pool, its unchanging surface faintly reflecting the arching ceiling of the room.

Many symbols were carved into the walls, and they held my focus for just a moment before my gaze was drawn back to Arthur. Despite being taller than the figure he now stood before, he looked like a child. I suddenly wanted to protect him, being awfully aware of the dangers of the path ahead. However, I could take joy in the honor shining clear in his face. My worries were dismissed as I joined the crowd in their silent reverence. He knelt. He appeared pale and thin as ever, but he was somehow stronger in the multicolored light of the cavern. He closed his eyes, the elder ahead of him beginning to speak. I didn't get the meaning of the words, but the tone held strength and compassion. It was one voice instead of the usual many, but it held behind it their support. I felt the power of generations, and that feeling only grew in intensity as his speech came to a climax. He called a few words out far more boldly, and the mass around me responded in increasingly agitated repetitions, stamping their feet on the floor and making high trills to the ceilings, pure joy and challenge that faded into the air. The cheering came to an abrupt end when Arthur stood..

The man stared at the crowds before him, tears in his eyes and more boldness I'd ever seen from him showing clearly in his stance, the tightness of his jaw, and the barest hint of joy pulling at the corners of his lips. He spoke, voice weaker than the chorus of cheers, but stronger then any I had heard from him. The room was silent when he finished, before he stepped forward. It seemed that some kind of invisible wall was shattered by the simple, everyday motion. The people erupted into chatter—to him, to themselves, and to each other, the stone again buzzing with the energy of a thousand thoughts. Not a single worker left without first pausing in front of him.

Some clasped his hand or his shoulder, some rested their palm on his forehead. Some whispered or whooped to him, short messages that overflowed with joy and celebration. It wasn't until the last guest had returned to their work that he collapsed onto one knee, both Ve and myself rushing to his side.

Arthur waved us off, a dry smile on his face. After a moment of tense silence, he spoke. "I think they forget how weak we humans are..I am." Muttering a vague translation for Ve, whose face broke into a half smile, he rose to his feet, mouth twisting into a small grimace. "They forget my wounds, though they do sort of stave away the pain."

He had been working in near-silence for days, and I had forgotten how eloquently he spoke, and the small reminder brought a relieved smile to my face. It remained there as he said his goodnights to the Triller, sending him off despite many chiding insistences and gestures to his head, his chest, the scar on his temple.

My smile remained on my face as I escorted Arthur back to where he slept, though he insisted on walking me back to my room as well. He paused at the doorway, and I quickly invited him inside. It didn't seem like I could sleep after the display, so I saw no trouble in another planning session to burn the midnight oil, literally. I may have missed flash-lights, just a bit.

We spent more time in thought before I spoke, figuring he didn't want to enter the room to just spend our working time in awed silence, as lovely as the echoes of celebration were.

"What did you say, that bit at the end?" I wondered aloud, perched on the edge of my bed with Arthur on the floor, back to looking like a nineteen-year-old man-child in his uniform coat and loose, pajama-looking slacks.

He smiled, facing me as he replied, "And when I return, may it be on the wings of freedom, to deliver you from this oppression, into the suns of peace. Poetic. Though, they don't exactly have a word for "oppression," or "deliver," or really "wings," not sure what I used for "return" either." His musings were not so poetic. Though, along with the laughter that burst out of him when he finished speaking, they made him seem suddenly and distinctly human.

With my new revelation that he might in fact be human, I allowed my curiosity to overtake my civil restraint. "Do they have last names?" My first question had to be easy enough, yes or no. Or so I thought, but I soon found out there never was a yes or no question if Arthur Keene had anything to say about it.

"Well yes, but no. Sort of. You see, they don't like to just limit themselves to their parents' bloodlines. Their last names are basically a translation of "Son or Daughter of all (FAMILY NAME) that came before me." He exhaled, blowing a bit of hair from his face. "For me, they simply said; Son of all."

He was tearing up a little, though I wasn't sure if it was because we were leaving, or he was tired and aching, or if it was because he had just been accepted into the community he'd lived in as a stranger for months in a deeper way than I had seen any human accept another. I chose to believe the first possibility because the second made me emotional, and I was tired.

But I remained awake, because there seemed to be still more information in his answer. "When two people mate, they can choose one name, combine the names, or create a new name." His insistence on detail somehow did not deter me, and I took notes as we continued to talk, the long day taking a toll on my spelling. Thus, we began a string of questions that kept us in conversation until I fell asleep at the foot of my bed, and he drifted off on the stone floor.

CTB 5

"His journey was almost at its end. His goals were almost fulfilled. His life, it was almost completed…Farrow dragged himself up those stones, forcing his battered body to take its place atop the mountain's peak. Even before he cast his gaze upon the still-smoldering villages, he knew the war was over. He could rest, knowing a new life awaited him."

[Will Durine, The Lives of Farrow Duke]

ARTHUR

I woke up before Nova, peeling my face off of the stone. She was splayed on her bed, so I left her to her sleep. Seemed more restful than mine. I never slept well, though I was comforted by the gentle noises of indistinct communications. Waking up for me was never pleasant either. Instead of a luxurious stretch and a bright new day, I was generally greeted with aching muscles and bolts of pain shooting from my injured limbs. Still, I got the unpleasantness of stifled groans and immovable extremities out of the way before Nova could wake up and feel bad about it. Stumbling groggily through the doorway, I pressed my shoulder against the wall to deal with the headaches. My limbs and my hands felt heavy, and my joints felt loose, a dull ache coursing through them as I left my arms loose at my side. More small rips formed in my already patched uniform jacket as I dragged myself down the wall. It used to be a nice jacket.

That's what I had once thought, at least. It was the really formal one, the one that scientists wore to broadcast.

I had once used it to prove my allegiance to the colony in my own broadcast. Now, it proudly displayed my place in the mines, thanks to many carefully styled edits. It was my favorite and basically only piece of clothing. The rest of my meager belongings had been in my pockets when I fell, or had been given to me. I literally owed these people everything, down to the loose slacks that swayed around my ankles as I moved.

I had just a few tasks to complete before I left. A few belongings to pack and a few more goodbyes to attend to. It now seemed so incredibly fast. Too fast. It was coming together all at once. I couldn't think of a time when anything was as urgent as leaving that planet. I can't now remember what I was thinking, not entirely awake yet. I finished up my packing in a haze of memory. I was remembering the night before, enchanting visions flashing across my mind. My thoughts were full of chanting and pools reflecting soft neon. My ears rang with the sounds of my new title. The name one final gift given to me by these people. It was one of the most awe-inspiring experiences of my life, lingering in my mind for the days it took me to fully process it. Nova had woken up and made her own sleepy stumble to my doorway by the time I finished packing up the rest of my things.

She looked absolutely exhausted. I guessed that she hadn't adjusted quite as well as I had to the noise of the mines. Of course, I had also spent a lot of my life in the colonies, which were near enough to feel the strongest sounds. We had a three week ship ride back to Earth stretching in front of us, and I wasn't sure if I could handle that much silence.

Though I would have plenty of time to sleep, and to think. Being alone with my thoughts. That's what I was excited for. Who doesn't love some good old fashioned isolation? At least I'd have her. I half smiled at the thought, peering seriously at the woman. I was squinting slightly, despite the softness of the room's lighting. "Morning. Long day ahead, are you ready?"

"We'll be in space. 'Day' is pretty loosely defined."

"Long time ahead." I turned my face back towards my work. I had things to do. Folding and refolding the small gifts of fabric and drawings the people of the mines had given me. Nothing as rare or valuable as jewelry or fine china, but the homemade forms of small wooden statues and the hand-woven texture of basic embroidery felt smooth under my fingertips as I skimmed my hands over their shapes. I felt her hand rest on my shoulder, and I tensed. I couldn't help it. But I soon calmed myself and turned to face her, her voice reassuring.

"You can't keep doing this to yourself. The ship's close, and you still have to speak with Ve."

I did, and I hated that. We hadn't had that much time together, with us both...occupied, but I loved the Triller like a brother, and the thought of saying goodbye to him hurt like a hot poker to the lungs. I was leaving him with a promise and a communication device. The comm would send us one or two messages before the scientists figured out the unfamiliar radio waves weren't a glitch, so long as he could get to the surface. And my promise was more important, a more definite reassurance than any device that I would return to him, "On the wings of liberation" as I had said before. Pretentious.

I finally folded and bent and packed my belongings into an acceptable fit, and I stood, bag in hand. The room was empty. Emptier than usual. And, it stood ready, waiting for someone or something to fill it with dreams and thoughts and joy. I wouldn't be a tragic mess any longer. At least, I decided that I wouldn't act like a tragic mess any longer. This silent vow was just another rod of steel in my spine, supporting my stance as I headed up towards the surface.

My footsteps echoed in my ears, and I pressed my palm harder onto the stones of the wall. The ridges dug into my skin. Nova strode confidently ahead of me, not as attached to the world as I was. We met Ve at the bottom of the stairwell, the two or three of us slinking along the rocks to avoid the gaze of those guards sitting above us. I don't suppose they cared much, however. It'd been almost a decade and a half without any successful revolt, so their focus had waned. I made a mental note. My feet were dragging, not for any rational reason, I just couldn't help but hesitate on my final march up the stairs. Final was just so, so final.

Ve stood in front of me, and Nova had shifted behind. Their positioning seemed instinctive, and as much as I admired their care, I was again pushing away feelings of being a kid again. A lonely kid, and a scrawny teen mocked for talking and thinking too fast and valued only for how he thought. I dismissed the thoughts and moved on to the top of the stairs. I was squinting even before we reached the surface layer. Even harsher than the torches, the glaring light at the top of the stairs assailed my eyes with its stubborn refusal to dim when my eyelids closed.

We slid out of the top and into the fields. There were a row of vehicles lined up next to the guard posts, and I knew most of the security codes. They used to change them monthly, but by then it was yearly. If that. "This seems simple" Nova whispered, gingerly batting the stalk of a plant away from her face. I squinted across the edge of the hole, spotting the two active guards resting in the shadow of the post.

"In any direction but the colony, it's tougher, but there's too much movement on that path to make it worth added security." I kept my voice low, dust tickling the back of my throat. The three of us slunk deeper into the fields, the scratchy plants arching high above our heads. The rubble of the ground dug into my knees through even the durable fabric laying like a second skin over mine. When we were near enough, I muttered the security codes to Nova, sending her off toward the car port to allow me a moment with my oldest friend.

He first rested his hand on my arm, slender, calloused fingers laid light on the jacket. I took a shaky breath as he shifted to lean his forehead on mine in the same gesture as when we first reunited in the mines. It was kind, familial, holding all the intimacy of true friendship. As we separated, I saw the faint reflections of past moments in his dark, mirrored eyes. He'd been called first when I'd woken up, caked in rock dust and chattering as he looked me up and down. When night fell, he'd show up and make me show him how much movement had returned, and check the wraps across my back. Once the danger of death had passed, he'd mutter "Rock wall" and gesture to the ridges that I could feel across my skin. Once I was up and moving again, he'd smile with his blunt teeth and comment on what a bad bird I made. I pressed the communications device into his other hand and moved back. I didn't cry, nor did I falter as I followed Nova. She'd managed to clamber in and was crouched behind the wheel, peeking above the dashboard. I couldn't drive something as basic as a golf cart, so I certainly couldn't drive an all terrain vehicle. Evidently, neither could my new, all-talented friend. She managed to punch in the security code while still crouched, and only shot up when the engine started. There was a bit of shouting back from the post, but whatever the words were, they got carried away in wind and dust and an engine roar.

I almost bounced out of my seat at each bump in the road, fingers gripping tightly to the sides and my legs flying up as I tumbled about the seats. It wasn't all bad, and I forgot my issues for just a moment. Whooping softly, and struggling to view the shaking scenery racing past my field of vision, I allowed my eyes and my mind to unfocus, for just a few brilliant minutes.

Then, the ride was over, quick. And we were fifty feet away from the colony, crouching by the garage, as close to the landing pad as we could be without attracting any attention. I'm not sure who would have bothered looking our way, anyway. Certainly no one cared about a peculiar shadow with an entire spacecraft setting down less than fifty meters away. Half of the colony's occupants must have left to figure out the cause of the unscheduled arrival.

I'm not quite sure, still, if I was more disturbed by the fact that I recognized half the faces, or that I didn't recognize the other half. My father led the crowd, his features already twisted into a mask of faux sincerity. I'm sure he had some drawn-out monologue about the tragedy of Nova's death. She had told me about the attempt on her life.

I kept thinking I had reached the limits of my horror, and yet my father still held the marvelous capacity to surprise me.

The ship finished its proper landing and the doors had just barely unlatched before Nova rose to her feet. I grabbed at her arm, hissing panicked commands to stop her. As against our goal her sudden reveal was, it was gratifying to watch her confident approach cut off my father's speech as soon as he opened his mouth to speak.

Dare I say, more gratifying was the strangled noise of panic he made when he saw her approach, scientists and explorers stepping aside to clear her path. That, in itself, was incredibly impressive. The pilot stepped out of his ship and stood behind her, arms crossed in a defensive stance. He had to be at least twenty years older than me, and he was a lot more intimidating than I could ever make myself. I didn't hear their conversations, with my head already ringing, but Nova's expression was a serene smile, and my father only grew more frustrated. She was brave, and brilliant, but she didn't know him like I did. She'd almost been murdered by him already, and I couldn't risk that again. Wouldn't. I still knew the broadcast codes, and I knew he prospered on his secrets remaining hidden. I'm still sure I was one of these secrets. So, that probably gave me some right to reveal his more evil ones.

I held the comm in both hands, staring at the image in front of me. We weren't live, Probably couldn't be, but I'd find out. Or bluff. I found myself unable to look at the codes flashing red, or the image, shrunk in the screen. I looked at my hands, to see if they trembled under the burden of my guilt. For once, they didn't. As I broke the treeline, one of the researchers stumbled back into the group, breathless.

The man spoke, breathless, "We were checking vital signs to make sure she—" He gestured vaguely over at Nova, whose face had soured, "To make sure that she didn't hurt the guards by the mines and-and we found…." His eyes met mine, just before he finished speaking, and the words shot back into his throat.

I'm not entirely sure I could describe the noise of shock he made, but it sounded a little like "Hhhhhn!" Faces began turning towards me, though my father's was one of the last.

He was the angriest by far, however, and the fury in his eyes almost made me step away, my muscles preparing to bolt on instinct.

I steeled myself. I kept my back straight and my grip tight. Thankfully, I didn't have to hold my stance for long, with my father's features dissolving into stunned confusion. He stepped towards me, the crowd parting around him, and I moved away, trying to keep my legs stiff despite the ache.

"Back off!" I raised the device like a shield in front of my face. "I know you tried to kill Nova, and I won't stand to watch you try again. You do anything, and it'll be sent to all the channels I can access." I spoke loudly, trying to look at Nova despite her being hidden behind his form. "And, that'll be a lot. I don't know if you heard, but you have a famous kid." My voice dripped with a dryness, my tone carefully casual and my free hand jammed into my uniform pocket.

"I know, Bud..Kid...Arty-Arthur." He seemed genuinely and satisfyingly uncertain.

"Arthur." I said simply, looking him seriously in the eyes. That was the first time I've ever done that, I realized. His eyes were green. Mine were brown.

"Arthur, this is your home, I'm your family. You can't just throw that away."

I scoffed, taking a step forward. Then another. Step by step, I reached the edge of the crowd.

"You threw my life away when you brought me here. You threw my childhood away. You discarded me when you pushed me down that mine."

"I didn't mean to...Your leg. You're limping." He actually sounded concerned, features softening. He did that

146

sometimes, after he got really angry. It made me feel bad to be mad at him, but this wasn't as light an offense as cracking my tablet.

I took a deep breath and walked past him. I moved to the pair backing me, pressing the comm into Nova's hand. I then spun and faced the man I had once considered to be my father, moving a step towards him.

"You ruined my life, neglected me, almost killed me over a business that enslaved people. Not beasts. Not creatures. PEOPLE." I gestured wildly in the vague direction of the mines, my face set in a scowl. "You don't care about me, or about anything. You lost that ability when your wife died, and your son became a burden rather than a child. Or before, maybe.." His mouth gaped open for a moment before he scoffed, angry.

"You're right," He finally conceded, shrugging. "You are a child. No one's going to listen to you. I'm offering you a job, a home, these mines to take over when you get this idea of mutiny out of your head, and you can't even be loyal enough to stay and live the life I earned for you."

I was shaken, but not broken, by his words. I think he said something else, but I can't remember it. I shook my head, pushing words out of a suddenly dry mouth. "You aren't allowed to do that. You aren't allowed to call me a child. I was supposed to be your child, and you forced me out of that. Sure, sure, I'm...I'm not loyal enough, and you want to know why? Because I'm not some dog, one so loyal as to follow you just because you didn't kick him as hard as you could have." I turned to face the ship, moving towards it. "I'm going to do what every parent wants their child to do. I'm going to change the world. And don't worry, your blood money should, your money should buy you a prison cell nice enough to watch it happen."

The door was open, so I went in, Nova rushing after me and the pilot remaining outside to finish the conversation with more necessary and less emotional subjects. Behind me, my father didn't speak. His face was red, and his hands were in fists and his lips had almost disappeared. I knew that expression, and I pushed it away. As soon as I felt far enough from the entrance to collapse, I fell, my muscles screaming and my head pounding. Then, angrily, I punched the floor, slamming the side of my fist into it with the force of frustration, concealed emotion, and just pure pain.

"Hey, come on." Nova knelt next to me and lifted my fist. She was smiling, I didn't know why. At the time, I couldn't fathom what she had to be happy about with the weight of our impossible crusade weighing heavy on my shoulders.

"You did it Arty-"

I cut her off. "No," I wasn't much for nicknames.

Holding her hands up in mock surrender, she continued, "You did it, Arthur. You made a promise we are going to fulfill. You aren't going at this alone, and we are absolutely going to change the world."

I was too tired to share her passionate enthusiasm, but I forced a weak smile, truly more of a grimace. "How do you do it? Stand so strong and so brave, I mean. In court, I assume, against them, even with me. It must be so exhausting."

Nova shrugged, sinking onto the floor next to me. "It is," She said quietly, staring at the blank wall ahead of us. "But if people don't listen, you either speak louder or stop talking, and I'm not going to stop talking."

I was awed. "You sent a scientist running. How did you do that?" I was curious, and it seemed like a helpful skill. Yet, instead of answering, Nova started giggling, her head in her hands. "I told him to get my bag from the colony. And he panicked."

I started laughing too, shaking helplessly. "That was your exit line, Really?" Amidst her laughing protests of "I need my things! We can't all survive on two rocks and a piece of string."

"..I didn't have any string."

We were still laughing when the pilot came back, making his way over to us and dropping a pair of bags next to her. He shook his head with exaggerated sternness, turning down the short hall.

"Bale, get your friend buckled in, we have a long journey and I kind of hate those guys standing outside the door."

I sobered up at that, Nova and I silently pulling ourselves up. She led me to what must have been the front of the ship, a small observational area with passenger seats laid out behind a space for two controllers on the dashboard.

I fumbled for a minute with the seat belt, but I felt ready. I stared out the front of the ship, knowing there were dozens of eyes watching us from the side and not wanting to consider the past. Instead, I stared into the future, feeling the rumble of the ship pass through me as we took off, ready to meet the stars.

Nova had been concerned with how I'd handle the noise of take off, I could tell by her expression, but I was honestly fine. It was only when we had passed the atmosphere and begun our glide through space that I began to have issues. It was far too quiet, the machine's noises just a hint of sound in the background. My head was pounding. I dealt with it for the first few hours as Nova showed me around.

The ship was efficient, made for fewer than ten people. It had cargo storage, an engine room, bedrooms, a common area, and a kitchen. Nova told me that there were ships just like mansions, or cruisers made for hundreds of people. Ships that were just for cargo, or smuggling illegal animals on earth. There were even some ships meant to freeze people or sustain generations to reach far away planets.

After the tour, she noticed pretty easily my discomfort brought upon by the headache tearing at my brain, and the ringing echoing in my ears. Even at almost lightspeed, the journey was three weeks, and I couldn't take the pain for that long. Well I could, but she didn't think I should have to. So, she found her personal communicator and a pair of earbuds, running through several types of music before we ended up just playing static. It was nice, and I wore the buds constantly, as a small comfort.

It was one of few however, joined only by Nova's books, my notes, and catching up on Earth news. Though, that was frustrating.

I hated the bed in my room. I sank into it like quicksand, and it made my bones ache. I ended up sleeping on the floor or at the desk. The desk was another comfort. Nova had brought plenty of clothes, but they weren't quite my size, so I ended up borrowing a few pieces from the pilot. He was taller than me, but I rolled up the bottoms of his denim pants and flannels. I found out that his name was Liam, and he really supported our cause. He had a daughter that he mentioned brightly-I wondered if my own father had ever talked about me like that.

Overall, the ride was uneventful, if not entirely pleasant. I read and wrote, planned with Nova, and was forced to readjust to Earth's greater gravity. Incredibly painful, especially with my mishealed bones, but I worked with whatever artificial gravity the ship could provide. I finally felt ready, or thought I was, until three weeks had gone by and Earth could be seen through the window of the ship. As I stared at its green and blue and brown—mainly brown— patterned surface, I realized that I was very, very wrong about how prepared I was.

THE CALL TO
UNITE

CTU 1

"As a child star, I grew up with my entire life laid out on display. Any friends I had, anything that I liked to do—it was all out there, waiting to be scrutinized by the masses… Sometimes, the spotlight was a warm glow, a shining beacon. Other times, it was more like the cold light of an operating room, and I was on the table, ready to be pulled apart."

[Elanor Firth, Flashing Lights]

NOVA

Arthur Keene is a fantastic person, a brilliant leader, and an amazing friend. To journey and bond with him during the three weeks we spent in space was incredible. The opportunity to grow to care for him was a gift. To actually care about him is absolutely terrible. He refuses to show anything but awe-inspiring strength and intelligence. Though he possesses both to great extents, the man won't let people think he is made up of anything else. He doesn't think people should be burdened with the pain he already bears.

That became clear very fast. We were an hour in and about at the end of the tour of the spaceship when I started asking questions. Though Arthur would never publicly clutch at his wounds, I had noticed his hand touching his head more and more often, as well as a stiffness in his expression that didn't fit our temporary state of safety. He walked with a limp, I knew that before. I had already noticed the lack of movement in his left shoulder and how he walked with exaggerated gentleness, favoring his left side.

What I learned after almost a half hour of coaxing was; he also got headaches. Bad ones. Also, his ears rang, apparently, and really badly in silence. So I set him up with a pair of buzzing, broken earbuds in my best attempt to make him comfortable. I had taken him off of the only planet he had ever properly known, so keeping him comfortable was the least I could do. Plus, I liked him. He was becoming my best friend, but I didn't know that yet.

Comfort was a more difficult task than I expected. The man is like some sort of stray animal. He refuses to sleep on a normal bed. The first night, I went to check on him and found him asleep in his chair. Not like he fell asleep while working. He *actually* dragged the chair to the middle of the room and fell asleep curled up in the seat. The next night, he was draped over the table like a Digital Era actress who just saw something worth fainting over. I made it a habit to find him each morning, either on the desk or the floor, or splayed over a seat in the small common room. Once I had to drag him out of the engine room. And, in his sleeping poses, he is freakishly flexible, and I had to get past that. Especially because he can hardly touch his toes when awake.

We all have odd habits. I also found out that Arthur writes on his skin without a care in the world. I've written a number on my palm, sure, but you'd never see lines of text across my forearm. It was a lot of effort to get that man ready for landing. Especially since I'd been in communication with the firm I was working with, and they had decided to tip off a news station or two. And those two had tipped off all the rest. Arthur was going to have to be seen in public, so it fell to me to get him looking like a human in his colony jacket and denim slacks he'd managed to get to fit him a little bit. That wasn't what I signed up for, but I cared for Arthur, and I was the only one of us that functioned like an actual adult.

We gathered by the exit, listening to the faint noises of people we knew were outside. It was a relief to see that the marks across his skin were still fading, standing out even less than his silver earbuds. The relief was,unfortunately, short-lived, as I finally gathered the nerve to peer out of the small window. The concrete of the ground surrounding the landing pad was barely visible under the swarms of reporters, cameras, and microphones poking above the mass like stark, black plants. They were about four feet down a small set of steps extending from the entrance and stretched across fifteen feet of parking lot between the plane and the car. Shouldn't be too long. Liam muttered a few vague excuses and retreated back into wherever he came from, leaving me and Arthur to stare at each other expectantly. He seemed to shove his nerves deep down, expression turning stony. I knew that he would volunteer to go out first, but I couldn't let him do that.

I pushed open the door and stepped out, posture fixed and smile professional. I had straightened my clothes out as well, stepping quickly down the stairs and waiting for Arthur at the bottom. He stared at the reporters for a second before lunging forward. My heart stopped for an achingly long second as he missed a step, catching himself at the bottom with a tight grip on the railings. The reporters began talking immediately, comments and questions flying around us.

His voice was calm and clear. "When I was four, my father, Ace Keene, came across a planet with intelligent life. When I was five, he took me from Earth and raised me on that planet, in a colony. I grew up there, lived and worked. The horrors of the civilization were hidden from me, as they were hidden from some of the researchers, and many of you, here on Earth. When I turned nineteen, the real purpose of the Janus colony was made clear to me. It is nothing but a business, and the lives of its people are nothing but the tools to be tossed aside." His tone was pleading, but his head was held high. Dignified.

"People. Not creatures, not beasts.'"

Seemingly unconsciously, he slipped his hair behind his ears. It showed the worst gashes that remained visible on his skin. "I would not have survived if not for the kindness and the civility of the beings that populate those mines. We, as a people, cannot let them remain in this state of suffering any longer. I hear you, I hear your questions, but the full extent of what needs to be known about me in this moment is contained in my relationship to the Chirosapiencidae. This is not some sort of social activist movement. This is a crisis that will spread across Janus and further if motions are not made to stop it where it is. "

At that, he broke, and whatever was keeping his words even fell flat.

"I came here, we came, we came here under great threat, and I face much greater, greater threats in the battle ahead." The small crowd of reporters had fallen silent. Arthur continued, his brow furrowing with focus, "This has to be said. I am not asking that you support me, I am only asking that you listen to me. I ask that you consider the plight of these people, and that you act on what you think—what you KNOW—is right. And now, if you'll excuse me…"

He took a small step, moving off of the stairs. That broke the silence, but I hurried to catch his arm and tug him through the crowd. His steps were heavy, and his feet sort of dragged.

We did make it to the cab, collapsing into the backseat. It must have been running, because we took off just a moment later. "Arthur," I asked, "How do you do that?"

He stared at me with a drawn brow, his head back over the edge of the seat, completely missing the headrest. He had given himself a cut and a shave while we were on the ship, stubbornly waving off Liam's attempts to help. Now there were small nicks reddening the skin of his cheeks and jaw, which had been mainly unmarked by scars. His hair hadn't been cropped into the stiff style of the colony, left hanging in locks and tufts around his ears. Teenage rebellion, I assumed silently, the wry observation bringing a faint smile to my face. It had gone past them when I'd first seen him, though, so more of a dignified rebellion. Or perhaps a way to hide a few of his scars.

"How do I do what, Nova?" Exhaustion rang through his voice.

That made me regret asking, but I was curious. "Talk like that. I took speech classes, but you spent years barely talking to people. Is it just in your nature?"

He shifted, looking away from me. "I did talk to people. I just found out at a young age that conversations are hard. While other people have this innate guidebook of conversational cues, I did not. I constantly have to think, to plan. So I ended up practicing public speaking without even knowing that I was. It's not tiring or frightening, and people don't stare and chuckle to themselves because you've gotten excited or frustrated and started to twist your hands together."

"Is it tiring to talk to me?"

"Sort of. But it's worth the effort. They weren't."

Then we were silent again. "Are you okay?" I asked, finally. He was poking at his knee through his slacks, legs bent outward.

"I'm not sure."

"Can you clap?"

Confused, he clapped his hands together. "Yeah?"

"Then you're fine."

The corners of his eyes wrinkled as he laughed. "My legs are sore, not my palms."

"You fell a hundred meters into stone, you can handle some muscle aches, can't you?"

He rolled his neck to face me, muttering, "I can feel my bones scraping together from how they mishealed. I don't need another injury."

I felt suddenly guilty. "Doctor's office when we get to the city, then."

"We'll be in Boston in a minute, and we can get a jet-cab for long distance to New York. Maybe you can sleep on the ride."

Arthur muttered a vague agreement, fixing his ear buds thoughtfully. He stared out at the airfield, cheek pressed against the window.He was the picture of thought for a moment before he pulled away, a sour expression forming.

"Window rattles a lot more than you'd expect." That was his only comment for the rest of the ride, as neither of us had any urge to speak. It was comfortable, though.

Arthur slept for about a half hour, I think. I'd spent the time flicking through news or staring down at the city, it wasn't common that I took trips long enough to justify the heights we were at. When we landed, I took my bags and he took his, and we both paused at the door of the apartment building.

I pressed the buzzer.

CTU 2

"We live, and in that; grow
As rain gathers into moonlit lake
From diamond drops and raining snow
Before the world of waters is scattered by the
quake
Of a man's boots, so small to his mind
Like ripples that can upturn any
A soul that's pined
Will find himself among many"

[Ben. I. Williams, Earthquake]

ARTHUR

The trip was long, but entirely uneventful. I used to take that as a good thing, but by then, it was as deafening as silence. I studied and prepared and fixed and fixed and fixed the earbuds Nova had given me. When we entered the building, my brain just went sort of numb, putting aside nerves and excitement and all those other natural reactions to change. That numbing emptiness was almost immediately replaced by an intense panic, as the door to the apartment swung open and a woman threw herself out in a blur of brown and blue and yellow. She and Nova both spoke loudly, voices growing louder and faster and higher. I jumped back, flinging myself onto the nearest radiator.

Their conversation eventually slowed, and the blur looked at me, her eyes narrowing as she turned back to face me. "You said he was alive." Nova nodded. "You said you wanted to help" Nodded again. The woman took a deep breath "You did **NOT** say you would bring him back here!" I was taken aback, sheepishly moving behind her. I had already been awestruck by her roommate, but the screaming really was a surprise.

"This is dangerous, Nova! You were threatened already, and that was before you dragged in this teenage, catchewed, basically fugitive! You know people will be after him." She gestured wildly while she spoke, so I slid back another step, still clutching the bag.

Nova sighed, shaking her head. "I couldn't leave him there. He actually has the possibility to make a difference, and I refuse to let that possibility die out. You know what it's like to deal with people who think they're better than you. His dad is like that, half the people on that planet are like that, and more than half of the people here. We're changing that, and he's going to headline. You know people care about what he does, what he says. You've seen the docs and the articles, and you'll see a new one soon." She finally pushed past the woman and entered the apartment, her voice fading off as I heard a bag hit the floor. I got another suspicious look before the roommate scurried after her.

I entered with a little more hesitation, feeling like an intruder, but it seemed ruder to just stand in the hall. I found myself in a sort of guest purgatory, standing at the doorway, back against the wall and bag clutched in both hands. I took a moment to take in my surroundings, making note of the window and doors. They said I was in danger, and no risk was worth taking. Though, if being comfortable wasn't too high a risk, that was the place I wanted to be comfortable in. The room wasn't big, but efforts had been made to make it comfortable. There was a small kitchen tucked behind a half wall, and a table next to it set out with fake flowers and two place settings. That did nothing to make me feel less like I was intruding. Most of the room was taken up by a sofa and a small table, a pair of bookshelves pressed to the wall. Small photos scattered the white wall next to two flags, the larger one striped yellow and red and blue, and the smaller one green and white, crescent to its left. National flags?

Despite the unity of all nations, many people still held pride in where they were born. I barely remembered. I knew I was from a big city, but not this one. I dismissed my thoughts of nationalism, as one must, and instead focused on the pictures. I'd almost moved close enough before not-Nova popped up in front of me. I stifled a noise of panic, raising my hands slightly. In defense or surrender, I'll never know.

"I'm Rosaline Kazmi. I've been best friends with Nova since we were children. I'll make it clear now that I do not support you putting her in danger."

A dozen protests and corrections rose to my tongue, but I kept quiet as she finished speaking. She was more than a half foot shorter than me, and very alarming. "Give me that bag and sit down. We'll make a bed for you on the couch tonight, but first, we are having a conversation."

I nodded and sat, fighting my urge to salute. That's a joke. I don't have any saluting instincts. Still, I did admire her dedication to her friendship. It was only terrifying to be on the other end of that protectiveness.

I waited in silent contemplation until both Rosaline and Nova had sat down, and then for a moment longer as they muttered between themselves. I heard Nova mention our doctor's appointment, but Rosaline cast a pleading gaze at her, and she immediately relented. That brought some questions to mind, but nothing urgent. After their quiet conversation had faded into silence, I straightened my back in a more prepared stance, waiting for her to speak.

"You now know my name, what is yours?"

I was a little confused, since Nova had told her, and she'd also said it was well known. I looked at the familiar face quickly, widening my eyes. She half nodded.

"Arthur Keene."

"Where did you grow up?

It was another piece of information I had announced, but I saw no point in not answering again.

"I was born on Earth, in a city. Chicago. We left when I was five. I lived in the Janus colony for fourteen years and the Janus mines from my first broadcast to about three weeks ago."

She nodded, satisfied. "And why are you here, on Earth, following a dangerous cause instead of living rich and safe in some family business? What put you on this path?"

My mouth went dry, my heart dropping into my stomach. I didn't have an answer for her, or for myself. All that I had done since my nineteenth birthday was reckless and dangerous and honestly, almost pointless. They were staring at me expectantly. I was supposed to know this. I was supposed to be sure of myself and my goals.

"Nothing, honestly. There wasn't a grand prophecy or a sword in a stone that told me I can do this. I didn't have people to tell me I could or should try and make a change. My own common sense is telling me to run at every turn. But, I saw something wrong in my world, and I wanted to fix it. It's not about doing something that puts me in people's minds or history books, I'm just someone who made a choice, same as anyone could have, and I will stand by my choice to help those who can't help themselves even if it does put me in danger."

After my declaration, my voice went quiet, even though I tried to muster power into it as I continued. "But I don't want to put others in danger. I don't want to put Nova in danger. If my actions put her in danger, I will find another way to free the Chirosapiencidae, and slow down the industrialization and the colonization and all that."

Nova looked shocked. Rosalaine, however, seemed satisfied with my answer. I looked at her instead. I figured Nova probably thought I was willing to ditch her after all she'd done for me. She was probably going to kick me out. I needed another person to stand as my landmark, another face for me to focus on. I hadn't actually looked at Rosaline before, too focused on other things or too afraid to actually look up at her.

She was on the smaller side, with me being a touch above average and her head ending at my chin. She had an oval-shaped head with soft, intelligent features. Her hair was dark and pulled back into a barely held together knot, strands falling onto the college shirt she wore. Her eyebrows were thin and arched above dark eyes, and when she had smiled at Nova, it took up half her face in joy.

I had been peering at her for a short while too long, blinking myself back into order as Nova stood. I felt my heartbeat ride in my ears as she stepped over to me. I blinked again, and her arms were around me, her hair scratching at my face. I didn't want her to let go. But she did, pushing away slightly to be able to speak.

"Sorry, I know you don't like touching. But, I had no destiny given to me, and I made the *choice* to join you. It is a choice I will make a thousand times over again."

Now, I felt as if I should have said something, but no words found themselves fit to crawl to my tongue. I didn't understand why she would say this, or, moreso, why she would mean it so deeply. Nova had a life before being swept into this cause, I didn't. She'd swept aside actual friends and family. Though, as much as I wanted her to have her life back, I was in no place to refuse help, as ill-advised as it was for her. She let go and took a few uneven breaths, my eyes tearing up as I looked at her.

I sat again, coughing awkwardly as Rosaline cocked her head to one side, the suspicion gone from her face. She and Nova stepped aside into another conversation, and I stared down at my arms, tracing the scars that I'd woken up with in the mines. I had to learn to get everything moving properly. I had healed wrong, and I knew it, but I could walk by now and hold things with my hands not shaking quite so much, and I had the earbuds for my headaches. I stretched my fingers, wincing painfully. There were a series of white and pink scrapes down my palm, left from when I'd dug through the rubble in an attempt to help the miners. I focused on the cuts as if I could heal myself by sheer force of will, create a miracle by thought.

More unlikely things had happened to me.

CTU 3

"The human body was created by nature and evolved in ages of advancement and growth. It is unbelievably strong and yet impossibly fragile. Of all the possibilities to break man, the easiest is found in the minds of children. More clearly, the minds of their parents. Neglect and emotional abuse can leave scars long after the marks of physical cruelty have faded from the skin."

{Union Edu, The Study of Man vol.2}

NOVA

I'd been waiting to see Rosaline for almost two months, six weeks of which had been absorbed by travel, of course. Travel which had given me too much time to think. To see her again was an immeasurable relief, if also a minefield of nerves. Somehow I managed to maneuver myself and Arthur through their meeting. There was just one hiccup, not one I'd anticipated. I didn't know how Arthur could believe that I would leave him to face the dangers of the quest we'd undertaken alone.

I left him to take a moment of peace as I spoke to Rosaline, a flurry of conversation that caught me up on what had happened in the two months I was away. When we finished our short exchange, I pulled her into a light embrace, my earring clinking against hers, before heading out of the apartment with Arthur popping up behind me just a moment too late. The sounds of him scrambling out after me brought a smile to my face, as honest and genuine as one could be.

It was an uneventful ride to the hospital. I wasn't sure how well it would end up if I took Arthur to the doctor's, and he was certainly injured enough to warrant an emergency visit.

We stepped into the waiting room just as the cheap screens played a clip of Arthur's entrance announcement. He rushed me over to one of the receptionists, a really pretty twenty-something who was staring at the video like she wanted to fly into the scene. I had to tap the desk to bring her attention to me, the woman falling over herself as she straightened up in her chair, her eyes meeting mine for a moment and then flying to the person next to me. That second action almost killed her. I don't say that in a threatening way; the receptionist did a double take before choking on air, her eyes blinking owlishly. I was almost sure she was going to tip her chair, she stood up so fast.

Didn't seem like anyone else was going to speak, so I did, my tone carefully calm, "Hi, we need to see a doctor. My name is-"

"Arthur Keene!" she squealed breathlessly. She honestly squealed. I didn't know people did that outside works of fiction. Jarring fact. At the moment, however, I was more annoyed than anything, my tone growing a little less civil.

"No, my name is Nova Bale. The patient's name is Arthur Keene, and he needs a doctor." I was a little curt, but he'd gone so long without proper medical attention, even if he did check himself in the ship's medical wing, and I didn't want him to wait a second longer than he had to.

He didn't see my point of view, casting a chastising look my way before he smiled at the receptionist, who was searching through her tablet.

"I can get you a doctor!" She exclaimed, before her pride shifted into confusion, "Sorry, right, why?"

"Bumps and bruises" Arthur trailed off halfway through the phrase, and she smiled sympathetically "yeah..what you're doing, though.."

"Well, I'm trying" he reaches out and took a clear, thick cased tablet from her outstretched hand. I glanced at it over his shoulder, scanning the questions about the patient. He lowered himself onto a plastic cushioned chair with a small grumble of complaint, I'd forgotten how clever he was. I was reminded when I returned from giving the receptionist the tablet. He'd taken apart his left earbud with his bare hands, the pieces laid out on the table next to him.

He looked up at me sheepishly, and I left him to his work as I distracted myself with tabloids on my own screen. The kid couldn't deal with his own public image, so I had to keep up. Besides, I liked them-particularly extravagant proposals and family scandals. A few minutes later, we were rushed down a plain white hall and into a plain white room. Personally, I hate hospitals. I make efforts to surround myself with color and life. I missed my pinks and yellows, as I had consistently through the six weeks of travel. Arthur seemed to be on edge as well, shifting uncomfortably on the crinkling paper that lined each stiff hospital cot. He avoided making noise for a few minutes, but grew visibly uncomfortable as we waited.

I leaned back on the wall, and he pushed at the papers, curiously listening to it crackle and rip. The door opened as he scrambled to straighten his back, staring at the doctor. She stepped over to me, extending her hand. "Doctor Raine, pleasure. I've just had a moment to look over your entry paperwork, and I noticed that under "Cause," you wrote-" She checked the tablet in her hand, "various injuries." The doctor looked up at me expectantly. "If one of you could explain..?" Arthur raised his hand slightly, the doctor turning to face him with a kind smile. He slipped out of his jacket, speaking with astounding calmness.

"I'm not going to assume you've seen anything else I've done or heard anything about me, if you don't mind. I do have various, and urgent injuries. I was pushed into the mines of the planet Janus CV197 and I fell against walls and outcrops before hitting the bottom. I was unconscious for a day and a half. If it hadn't been for the planet's lower gravity and the native species' attempts to slow my fall, I wouldn't have woken up at all. When I did, there were a good amount of bruises and gashes, concentrated on my left side. These forced me to learn how to move properly again, and even worse than that, fractures, dislocated joints, and major injuries that I didn't have the tools to heal correctly. On top of this, head trauma led to some debilitating headaches and some form of tinnitus. I've handled most of these issues, to the best of my ability. However, I've been experiencing some pain since we landed on this planet and that's something I'd really like to deal with." " He smiled politely, the doctor looking taken aback.

"I'll start with the easiest question I can think of for us to digest all this information." Her fingers burst into a flurry of motion as she typed the new information into the tablet. I'd been alarmed, when I first met him, at how casually he described tragedy, with no stammer or hesitation. Particularly his own. However, I'd moved past it, and she'd recover.

We waited patiently until she continued her thought. "You self-diagnosed all these injuries and…" she gestured around vaguely, "everything. What led you to that conclusion?"

Arthur blinked slowly, looking confused. "Well, the gashes and bruises are visible, the internal breaks and aches have been very clear for months, the headaches have brought me to the floor in pain, and I know the symptoms of tinnitus, and I match them because I can hear the universe screaming."

"I'll still need to check that myself. I'm just going to look over some of your range of motion, visible scars, and ask you a few questions to start us off."

I checked my messages while they spoke, only glancing up at the slight, pained grumbles that Arthur muffled as his knee bent a bit farther than it was able to. They finished in about ten minutes, and the doctor grabbed her screen.

"I'll go see what I can do about your out of date medical records and set up a scan."

"Thank you!" He called politely, the doctor nodding as she left.

"That was showing off," I commented as the door closed.

Arthur's posture fell, and the smile faded. "I don't like hospitals. I don't want to stay longer than I have to, and I *know* what's wrong. I know exactly what's wrong with me. I just can't, I can't fix it, not well enough."

The next few hours were spent in a half dozen hospital rooms. I was in and out, ending up in the hallway when they finally finished up. You weren't supposed to stay there, but we argued it was an absolute necessity that I be nearby, and the situation was exceptional. Plus, I couldn't leave him alone. The hospital was public, the Union against Arthur. There were a thousand possibilities that flashed between my eyes, each one more terrible than the last.

The people that talked with me seemed to think of him as simultaneously fragile and made of steel, something unreal and divine, all powerful but ready to break apart.

When all the tests and scans had run their course, and I'd been summoned in from the hallway, we stood in front of the doctor. Arthur's shoes were on the ground next to his neatly folded jacket, and he had lost almost a half an inch from it. I was still shorter. By a lot. But it was notable none-theless, even saddening when paired with how tired he looked, pale again in the lights.

"Ms. Bale, I can share some of this information with you, but the rest of it will have to be shared by Mr. Keene himself." I nodded, shrugging it off. I was sure he'd tell me everything, so it didn't matter much if the doctor did. "Great. To start, we did find many internal injuries that didn't heal as they should have. This is presumably due to the planet's gravity. We can fix these injuries."

Arthur exhaled.

"Unfortunately, to do so, we will have to re-injure you, so they can heal correctly. Given that we can only complete this process with a few injuries at a time, you will likely be close to incapacitated for a few weeks, maybe months. At least. I can give you more information, but I'll need your preliminary approval now. Are you willing to undergo this process of healing?"

And again, he was holding his breath. A few seconds passed before I saw him shake his head, eyes downcast. "Chirosapiencidae are killed and maimed and torn away from their families each day. They don't have the luxury of time. So I don't either. When I finish my fight, then I'm sure I can get everything together."

The doctor nodded, looking disappointed with his choice. Still, she continued dutifully, "I'll prescribe painkillers, and we'll be in touch with a more detailed report. For now, all I can suggest is to avoid anything physically strenuous, and to consider your other options more seriously." He nodded, and she again continued. ''Your gashes and scrapes seem to be scars, if anything, so no worries there..' The woman swiped on her screen "You do have tinnitus, and we can get you a better hearing aid. Your headaches are not only caused by the trauma, but also by your brain developing on a planet that, to the best of my knowledge, produces a frequency different from that of Earth. Your earbuds should also help with that, and we'll find a specialist for you with a more permanent fix. Now, I think Miss Bale should step out, just for a minute."

Walking back to the waiting room, my mind went to all the worst places. I quieted my thoughts with the reassurance that he would tell me when he could. That was all I could do.

I was wrong. Arthur left the room in silence, walked into the waiting area in silence, and followed me to the street in silence. The only noise was the soft clicking of mechanical parts as he fiddled with his earbuds in the taxi. I waited, wanting to give him time, but I couldn't help commenting as we grew closer to the apartment, "Do you want to tell me what she said? You don't have to, but we'll be back soon."

He leaned back against his seat, his eyes closing. I didn't want to pressure him into speaking, but he seemed almost ready to tell me. It was a solemn moment.

He did, eventually, speak, straightening his back and clasping his hands in his lap. I waited expectantly, keeping my expression neutral. "This last issue is a lot different than the others. It's not solvable. It's really bad." My heartbeat sped up, all the worst possibilities springing back to mind. My breath caught in my throat; otherwise, I would have moved to comfort him. The man cast his eyes downward, his shoulders lowering. "The doctor thinks I've got anxiety. And, the panic, it's why my heart starts beating, and the world starts swaying sometimes…I'm just, just messed up, from my father, from the move to the planet, from falling into the mines and from all of it." He looked angry. "It just messed me up. It wasn't supposed to. If nothing else, every-thing I've gone through was supposed to make me strong-"

He brought his fist down on his leg, jaw set angrily. "It's just so USELESS."

I'd never seen this intensity from Arthur before. He'd been sad, even angry, but it had been carefully controlled and used for something practical. I'd admired him for that. Now, I admired him even more. I'd known that he mainly grew up alone, and he didn't spend much time with his father, but I hadn't known how he held the weight of his childhood, or why he insisted on putting all his emotions to some sort of use. He didn't know how to deal with them; no one had ever shown him. Finding out there was something medically wrong with his mind, something that wasn't a problem to be solved, I knew it had to be killing him.

"I'm not supposed to have a weakness up here." Arthur pounded the heel of his hand into his forehead, and I sprang forward, catching his wrists. I immediately regretted it, and let go as his hands fell limply into his lap.

He finally looked up at me, and he wasn't crying, though his eyes were shining with tears. He just looked so hopeless, I almost curled up into a ball and gave up. If he carried all that pain inside of him, I could deal with seeing it, with taking as much of it as he would let me.

"This isn't a weakness. It's a challenge, but it's never stopped you from doing spectacular things. When I was nineteen, not long ago, I was half studying and half curled in my pajamas watching digital era movies. You're unbelievable, and we'll find ways to get you through the attacks. We. Your dad may have broken you up, but I'm here to pull together the pieces. If you feel like the world is closing up around you, I'll be there to push the walls away. If you wake up with nightmares, I'll sit by the bed or floor you're sleeping on, and I'll wave a flashlight around until the shadows fade. If your mind flies back to that colony, I'll pull you home again."

I watched him wipe his eyes, dark and watery. There was more to say.

"If you just can't deal with the people around you, I'll throw my arms in the air and kick my legs up until they all run away from us."

Arthur wiped his eyes again, half chuckling. "Us," he whispered, and I nodded.

"You've signed on for more than you think...the head trauma gave me short term memory loss. Forgot to tell you, with all the bonding moments" A smile flashed onto his face before fading back into a mask. "It's really minor, and there's treatment, but you'll probably have to carry around a notepad or a spare tablet, so you can write me reminders. My brain is important, it's all I've got, so my father just had to spoil it as soon as it didn't work for him anymore." He looked so despairing, but he brushed it off, again fixing his posture and forcing a breath into his lungs, though he still looked quite a bit too unsteady to speak

"You can forget my name, and I'll still follow you to the end of the universe," I promised.

"I swear I'll never forget you."

CTU 4

"Life is a series of revelations and changes, choices and 'plot twists' that make up our experience and our identity. There is no true peace, even in contentment, for that is not living, it is simply being. Any pause in life is not a rest, it is simply the calm before the storm."

[Adai Vernon, The Calm Before]

ARTHUR

I will not speak about the hospital visit. I won't talk about how it felt when the doctor told me that there was something wrong with me. I will never speak of the cab ride after, or how I didn't even plan to tell Nova about the memory loss because as minor as it was, I was afraid she'd think I would forget everything and be a helpless dead weight. How I squeezed it in at the end, when I was hopelessly confused and frustrated, and nothing in the entire world seemed worth keeping from her. I still don't know why she said the things she said, why I didn't understand because I had long ago figured out that not being "normal" was a weakness I couldn't afford. I won't talk about any of that.

All I will mention is that Nova Bale is an impossibly kind human being who I would not have survived without. She was my first human friend.

The problem, at the time, was that she was caught between two people, two paths. Rosaline was her past, and had known her since they were children. I'd known her for a month and a half and was incredibly different from the sweet, if completely intimidating young lawyer who she lived with. When we arrived back at her apartment from the hospital, it seemed she would have to mix two worlds, and that's never a simple task.

It started with the three of us sitting in a vaguely circular shape, my tears just dried and my hands laid in my lap. We stared at each other for no less than a minute in silence, a foot away but worlds apart. Nova broke the silence.

"We should all get to know each other, we'll be living together for a short while at least so you two—" she gestured vaguely, "—questions."

I looked up from my lap to see that Rosaline had done the same, the two of us pausing in a moment of uncomfortably extended eye contact. She had grilled me earlier, so it seemed to be my turn to ask.

"Where did you and Nova meet?"

"There's communities set up for orphans of war. Places for high ranking people to dump the kids whose lives are ruined by their actions. I was born in Pakistan and lost my parents when I was eight. I went around a bit before I ended up in Colombia, in the community where Nova's biological parents are caretakers."

Nova spoke up, "My grandparents are from Guyana, but my dad's family was Colombian, and there were some community roots there, so that's where they ended up."

"So you're siblings? Adopted?"

"No. There's more than one family. But it's a close community. Everyone's looking for attachments at an unsteady time."

"So are you two..." I had found my words catching in my throat "romantically involved?"

Nova, who had opened her tablet and gone to work at the end of the table, looked at Rosaline with an amused expression creeping onto her face. Rosaline glanced at her, before back at me. I regretted asking the question, but I was considering a personal investment in the answer, so it had to be done.

Rosaline finally shook her head, seeming to consider her words. "No. We were "romantically involved" in high school, then we broke up and things got a little awkward. We sort of stopped talking. Then, small community, figured out we were going to the same school and left the past behind. Had to grow up sometime, you know?"

I nodded agreeably. In fact, I did not know. I didn't know the dramatic highs and lows of high school. However, I wasn't so socially self-sabotaging as to mention that.

"Are you homesick, Arthur?"

"Already? Not nearly. I've got a few good memories of the colony, and the mines are a deeply rooted part of me by this point...." I tucked my hands into my pockets, "whether that's good or bad. Are you homesick? Do you miss where you were born, or where you grew up? The food, the culture?"

I saw Nova look at her, her hands held in her lap. I guessed they didn't talk about that much.

"Well, Arthur. Where Rosa grew up and where she was born were very different. Where we grew up was pretty similar to here, if a little smaller and less crowded...but the culture...." She seemed to be struggling to explain something that was only meant to be learned through experience. "Because of a lot of union mandates, I spoke English first, grew up with a lot of American media, ideas, etcetera. I went out of my way to learn any Spanish..my parents and grandparents were caught in the middle of all that culture shift..some of them have some real fear about being proud. We had museums, but they made our traditions into something of the past. Wasn't until the last few years that a lot of countries are fighting back for their traditions and their languages, but the second wave left a deep impact."

Rosaline shifted uncomfortably, picking up where Nova left off. "I grew up in one of those few groups that were more untouched by the Union. They were still religious, still held deeply to their traditions. When the Union people came, they truly did think it was a kind of freedom. I don't know if I miss that home. I haven't been back. I've looked it up, though, and like Nova said, there is a fight to reclaim all that." She exhaled slowly, "Maybe that's the fourth wave.

Could be happening. Either way, we like it here. We went to university here, and it's loose and mixed and bright." They were both silent

She did speak again, so I, thankfully, wasn't forced to. "On the topic of university, do you have any actual schooling? High school, university, did you have a tutor?"

"I went to kindergarten. I was *really* bad at it. To be fair, my mom was dying, but still. Then I got access to an adult screen, and I made my own lessons. At fifteen, I got into so,e university courses, and I've gotten my specialized degree since then. I didn't have a lot to do beyond studying. I also learned very specific bits and pieces of knowledge through the staff of the colony. I'm not very good at memorization. I like problem solving. Anatomy, working in a lab...I did a lot of that after I turned sixteen."

"Well, now I think you're just bragging." She seemed to be trying to keep a smile off her face, and I liked making her smile, even if it wasn't quite there.

"Maybe I was. Are you impressed?"

"Not quite, and I think that's your question."

I gasped in mock offense, shaking my head. "I'll never play this game with you again!"

She laughed, suddenly and brightly. "Then I'll make the most of this round, Arthur."

We talked as the minutes dripped into hours. The later the time got, the more amusing her replies seemed to get, and mine as well, as we were both helpless heaps of laughter by the time Nova had drifted off to sleep. The two of us dragged her to bed, leaving her slumped over her sheets. I was exhausted, and it was dark, though what I could tell of

183

her room was bright and jumbled and lively. Soon after, we had gotten back around the table, and our questions became less coherent and more wildly entertaining. I learned a lot about her, I remember now, though I remembered very little of it as I woke up the next morning, after an hour of sleep, at dawn's first light, piled on the floor with my legs kicked up onto the chair I was sitting in.

It was a solidly unpleasant morning. Aching, as well, but in the most fantastically normal way of twenty-year-olds. A moment after my eyes opened, I drew myself to my feet, holding onto the edge of the table. And then I realized my leg was numb, and I crumbled like sand in rain, stifling a shriek as my back hit the floor, the chair I'd fallen asleep on landing on top of me. It was in this state I stared at the ceiling of the kitchen and considered how my life had changed. I moved to my feet a half an hour later, grabbing at my earbuds and fumbling them deeper into my ears to ward off the headache that'd been digging its way into my brain. I moved through the room, squinting out the window. Not too much of a view, but different from the dusty fields of Janus and the vast emptiness of space. I quite liked it. Except the sky. There had been no stars the night before, and the sunlight was faded.

I had moved to the counter and made myself a cup of tea before I heard footsteps approaching me from behind. Without thinking, I lowered my head, bending my back to take up as little room as I possibly could. Nova came up next to me, leaning on the wall.

"Morning. I woke up at two last night, and all I heard was a sort of shrieking laughter. Did Rosa take you drinking?" she questioned.

"No, I don't think I'll ever drink. It only causes bad things. I haven't slept properly in forever, and I was delirious. Best laugh I've had in ages, though."

Nova half nodded, head in hand as she opened up a set of slides on her tablet screen. "Right now, we've got two plans we need to get written out."

I found myself confused but remained silent, perched on one of the seats around the table. She swiped up one, carefully gesturing to the title: "Number One-Getting Mr. Arthur Keene into the public eye and making his cause one that people know and care about." I nodded, that was important. I couldn't imagine what the other plan was. She spun her tablet around, smiling widely. "Plan Number Two- Getting Mr. Arthur Keene a social life and dragging him around the city, if not the country because he needs a LIFE." It took a moment for me to process, half asleep as I was. "Long title- wait, NO!"

Before the protest even rang out, I was lunging for the tablet and sliding it under my arm. I retreated to the other room with Nova hot on my heels, less than graceful as she knocked a chair aside. Rosaline shot up suddenly, accidentally swatting my mug off the table just as she dove at me. I shielded myself with a pillow, throwing it at her as I rolled off the couch. The tablet was still clutched tightly to my chest. It smacked Rosa in the face, her arms already raised in mock surrender, and I pulled myself off the floor, checking the device for injury.

Thankfully, I wasn't holding it out, because seconds later, my face hit carpet. Rosaline had crept around the room and taken me down, the tablet flying out of my hand. I muttered some sort of vague complaint, rolling onto my back and spitting out an unhealthy amount of whatever the carpet was made of. My leg creaked a little in complaint, and my rib stabbed at my stomach. Rosaline's knees were pressing into my chest as she accounted for me rolling over. They had possibly punctured my spleen. I didn't see why a spleen was necessary. It was just there for pretty and shockingly strong young lawyers to impale with their painfully bony knees as their friends made plans to force you into a social life.

I groaned hoarsely, blinking the light out of my eyes as I stared up at her. She wasn't looking at me, laughing as Nova took the tablet. She'd just woken up, and her hair was still half up, the other half tumbling down her neck, with small tendrils framing her face. I was mesmerized, and also half blinded, by the light that shone out from a lamp behind her head like a halo. But it's a good lesson I've learned, to never stare into light bulbs, no matter how taken you are with the person sitting in front of them. She finally removed her knees, excusing herself into the other room. I deflated and folded onto the floor with an audible noise of complaint. Nova stepped over, nudging me with her foot.

"Come on now, you've got to make yourself another cup of tea, it was a casualty of war!" The last bit was exclaimed, with extra passion and pizzaz. I managed a smile, but was suddenly a bit tired.

Now, on the journey from Janus, I had made attempts to map out and understand every part of the ship. In the recreational and living areas, there were large, rectangular screens, framed in shiny black. I hadn't had a television, hadn't really wanted one. Still, I watched. I watched old digital or nuclear era movies, early or mid starflight films, and even those that proudly displayed "NEW" in bright red letters. The drone of the characters, along with the white noise of my earbuds, helped me focus better. I didn't pay attention...mainly. There were one or two that caught my eye, a flash of love beyond passion, a glimpse of heartache, a bare moment of simple, normal life. I quite liked the families at the start of the movies full of curses and killers. They were fascinating, before all of the annoying screeching and screaming and fake blood.

I had learned from all these bits and pieces that families play-fight, smack you on the back of the head or steal your breakfast, or, I suppose, chase you across the room for the device you're holding. I knew what family was, in theory and by definition. Friendship as a concept, closeness as a nearly-faded fact. I just didn't know the truth of it, the reality of warmth in your chest and a sort of pleasant calm in your mind. There was a consideration to be taken from that, but Nova had opened up the lists again, so the thoughts fell from my mind, as thoughts are inclined to do.

I slowly made my drink, lingering on the process before trudging over to the table and taking a seat next to Rosaline. "What's the first step?" I asked, pulling dramatic resignation into my voice.

"Getting you some actual human clothes."

I slumped onto the table, staring at the city through the nearest window. "What about the other list? Let's focus on my less personal points. Please, Nova." The lightness of the room became denser, and her smile faltered. I did want to stop talking, really. "I came to Earth for one reason, as cheerful and normal as you think this trip could be...."

"You're right. Step one of the other list is a lot more specific." The dryness in her voice made me feel as if the step wasn't going to be one I'd take joy in, but I squinted at the words anyway. "1. Get clothes that don't look like something a student would wear during finals."

"I don't know what students look like during finals; my schooling was a combination of self teaching, artificial intelligence, and the Internet."

Nova laughed loudly. "I've heard the basics of how you grew up, but now seems like a fine time for you to tell me more."

I shrugged vaguely, sipping my tea as I scanned the list, backwards.

"We can get everything you need in three stores. And I'll take you to a museum after. You need to learn how to survive in the public eye like a human."

"That's speciesist."

"You are a human, and either way, humanizing anything brings out feelings of empathy in society, so you're going to wear a sweatshirt and jeans, and you've got to be positive about it."

"Two stores, and I'll let you make me a social media account, #4 on getting into the public eye."

She closed the screen, throwing her hands in the air. "Fine. I want to protect my savings anyway, so two stores is better."

I would never make her use her own money, and I couldn't believe she would think that. "I have a savings account, from my mom." I hadn't mentioned her yet. But, Nova didn't seem phased, continuing to scan through men's clothing stores. I had let my attention fade before I was again forcibly pulled into the real world when she stood, chair squeaking sharply. She strode out of the room, and I moved to check the lists in more detail. A minute later, I hit the floor again.

Now, sidenote. It is not the force of a sweatshirt hitting one's face that can knock one out of a chair. What can knock one out of a chair is an attempt to jump to one's feet out of a stool, and flipping back over it because it doesn't have a back. Definitely hurt.

Nova followed the sweatshirt, a bundle of fabric in her hands "Are you okay?" As I nodded, she helped me to my feet "Can't have you in your colony jacket, because of obvious reasons, and your Triller clothes look like Mid Crisis pajamas, and that's saying something."

She handed me a pair of slacks.

"Put that on, and no one will go out of their way to speak to you. Now, enjoy your tea, and I'm going to go get dressed."

I held the piece of clothing up. It was clearly labeled with the name of some activist group, and the back held bold letters that spelled out " VOLUNTEER." Brilliant.

I chuckled and pulled it on over the heavily tailored short-sleeve from Liam, which I would be thrilled to change. I hadn't felt like myself since I'd gotten on that ship, holding a deep-rooted uneasiness close to my chest. Lopping off half the hair that had grown during my time in the mines had been a relief, made more satisfying by getting to choose to leave it past my ears. I had kept it uniform short since I was five, and there had been bigger problems than a haircut in the mines. More than the look, or the unfortunate ability to snag myself on any hook or edge, I loved the ability to make a choice. To an extent.

When we had flown into the city, we had passed loads of buildings, and hundreds of them were shops. It seemed impossibly complex. Thankfully, I had a friend. She emerged again from her room in time for Rosaline to wave us away, as she attempted to simultaneously tie her shoes and button a blazer.

"She's already late," Nova muttered to me as we closed the door.

She moved quickly, ignoring crowds of people larger than I'd see in years. One street had more than the whole colony. Her steps were short, but determined. On the other hand, I was dragging my feet before we even got past the window displays. There were a lot more options than I had expected, and Nova went ahead, muttering something about finding more formal clothes.

It seemed like she was having doubts about helping me like she was, but without her help, I'd be a deer in headlights, and they'd find me a week later, collapsed in a pile of shirts, none of which I had bought.

To be fair, it was feeling like that might happen anyway. I stood in the doorway until a few other customers nudged past me, and I muttered apologies, darting away. A man gave me an odd look. With another apology, I slid deeper into the store. How was I supposed to know what sort of clothes I liked? Sure, after The Crisis, fashion was pushed aside in favor of loose, plain-colored clothing, meant to promote equality and unity. Then, people had gotten very Second Wave, and fashion had become rigid and traditional.

Then there was a reform, supposedly, and it'd become a lot less defined. I had studied history, and I knew the ages. There were tunics and vests and blouses tailored out of Medieval Europe, and other more ancient societies. They had a place again, mixed among nuclear age suits and bright skirts and clicking heels. Pre-Digital sweaters and jumpers were torn apart and stitched into the Digital graphic short-sleeved shirts and jeans. All pulled apart and pushed together and mixed and made new; it was so very human.

I didn't yet quite know what I liked. All the options seemed unnecessary, but I reminded myself that anything able to bring joy can't totally be. I reached out, letting the world fall into blocks of color and vague white noise as my fingers skimmed the clothes. I ended up with a pile of fabrics, not quite sure when or by what standards I had chosen them. I figured that I'd find out eventually, and I really wanted to get to that museum. So I held the clothes limply, not paying a lot of attention except to know when to move forward in line.

"Your hand...?"

I was yanked into reality and realized I had handed the clothes to the cashier.

"To pay? A card, chip or print work as well," The man encouraged. He had nice eyes, and for a moment my thoughts shot to what an Earth relationship would be like. Then the total was flashing green on the register, and I blinked at it before lifting my hand and pressing my finger into the print scanner. It beeped, I clicked in six numbers and drew my arm back. Being aware of my surroundings also made me aware of my headache, which was unfortunate. Thank goodness for conscious thought.

"Great. Have a nice day!" He was bright and cheery, despite my time-wasting struggles and the growing line behind me.

I smiled grimly and grabbed the clothes. Nova met me at the door.

"How'd it go?"

Her voice was curious, and she looked pleased at the bag swung over my arm.

"To be honest, I don't really remember. And I don't mind. Can we go to the museum now?"

"I can't believe I had to bribe you with a field trip," she scoffed, though a smile remained planted on her face. "Come on, next store. I want to get to the museum as much as you do."

CTU 5

"In theory, being injured is a tragedy. But, in reality, it is just a side effect of being alive. Life is full of wounds, big and small, real and figurative, that serve as the world's way of making sure that we don't break, or fall, that we survive. Or maybe, the world is not this kind, and all of these are its attempts to kill us."

{Jack Wachjab, Essential Theories of Modern Medicine}

NOVA

When Arthur met Rosaline, all of my choices became incredibly real. Sure, I knew I made the choice to go to another planet, to protest a movement with deep-rooted support from high powers. I knew I had found a man who was supposed to be dead, and I knew I had brought him back to Earth. However, that felt like some other life, like it was removed and I'd suddenly end up back in my real life, not making a difference. Because it couldn't be possible that I was. That wasn't the kind of thing that happened to me.

Finding a lost leader and fighting for an alien species, being threatened by elegant government spies with suit vests and robotic hands wasn't the sort of thing that happened to normal people, to teacher's pets with both parents and a half dozen siblings. It happened to pretty, pale girls in YA novels who had blue eyes and blonde hair and never got hurt and could lift weapons half of their weight, which was a hundred pounds, on average.

Bringing Arthur to the apartment I'd been living in since I came to the city, seeing him among the small comforts from shops I'd been to once, and pictures of my family hung too high up to fit the space on the walls, that was wholly different from any other context we'd been in. It made everything unsettlingly real. When Rosaline started interrogating Arthur, things should have begun to feel more normal—less removed from real life. They didn't. It all felt even more unreal, and I felt as if I was wading through a dream. I had made a lot of choices, and everything had to end well, it absolutely had to. If it didn't, I wasn't sure what I'd do.

The Crisis Remembrance Museum. We were trying to keep another planet from being infected and industrialized, so he deserved to see the results from when it couldn't be prevented. Plus, with his limp, I wasn't going to make him walk far. I silently took one of his bags, not wanting to point out that I still knew his left arm hung wrong, and he had to be aching in more ways than one, after having given up the chance to get it healed right.

The museum was quiet, a few hushed conversations and the respectful voices of tour guides beyond the lobby walls. The timeline, a long white wall with a black line flashing across it. Evenly spaced slashes separated it, with a date below and neat, square, letters spelling out important events above.

It started in 48 Digital Era (D.E.), when the environmental decline was officially declared a Crisis. Nothing changed, and a year and a half later, the damage was irreversible. Less than a decade—and about two steps—later, we came to the end of the Digital Era. Everyone, even those who had earlier decided to value money over land and life, had been alerted to the problem by all the forces of nature. Seasons became unpredictable and irregular, weather disasters sprang up anywhere at any time, farming started failing, and being born with any respiratory issue was a death sentence. After the trees were destroyed in pursuit of industry, and the air hung with plastic and other pollutants, after the cross into what we remember as officially the Crisis Era, the descriptions got darker. Those with the money launched themselves into space, those with the brains formed a secret group and locked themselves away, cultivating an elite group with a distinct quest to save humanity.

The rest, not rich enough or exceptional enough, lived in small groups of destroyed buildings, with not enough food and the constant threat of war or disease. We, as a species, almost wiped ourselves out. Then the first non-microscopic alien was found, and fear overwhelmed the "survival of the fittest" attitude that had overtaken humanity. Less than a decade passed, and then the world was forcibly pulled together. Dams and houses and factories and power plants and whole chunks of cities were cleaned out, with vines and rocks and the collected marks of nature completely erased. Borders were established back in the States, and all of the nations were corralled under the ambassadorial system, by force or choice. Even those who had flown away when things got bad found their way back, and the Starflight Era officially began.

Landfills stuffed with plastic were cleaned, and what wasn't usable was shipped off the planet. Colonies were established as the population regrew, by reproduction or "test tube babies." Everything was looking good. Then humanity kicked into its old patterns, and the same mistakes were made again. The only change was that there were more planets infected, more lands to strip and destroy. History fell into its normal habit of repeating itself as the peace and equality dissolved into corruption, greed, industrialism, and a divine right to expand, claimed in the name of science instead of the name of God. New resources were brought in, new forests were destroyed, new plants were stripped of their fossil fuels, and the earth was hidden from the stars by fog.

We went deeper into the museum, each time displayed before us. The videos and statistics and holographic visuals showed burning trees and warring factions above serious labels that trapped the horrors of decades in fewer than a hundred words. We didn't speak. The room was remarkably quiet, until the silence was broken by the echoing voice of a tour guide. I caught Arthur by the sleeve and guided him to the group, finding our place near the back of the tourist clump.

Arthur adjusted his earbuds, which let out a shrill crackle of static beyond the usual white noise. It rang out loudly, shattering the contemplative peace like a bolt of lightning. It must have been painful. The man just in front of us glanced over, and I noticed his eyebrows furrowed, though I believed that to be the end of it. He moved away slightly after that, and kept casting arched-eyebrow glances at Arthur

I kept an eye on him, though he utterly disregarded me. His hair was just past being called graying, and he walked alone, with the slow steps of an older man.

We moved on, passing into the rooms of larger exhibits. The group paused in front of a large map, clustered with red dots. The guide turned to face us, her voice respectfully hushed

"This illustrates sites of particular tragedy in the early states of the Crisis: Tsunamis, storms, fires, and other natural disasters, before the fighting and the sicknesses spread." She reached up, pressing one of the dots.

A mechanical voice rang out, "In Southern California, wildfires-" Out of the corner of my eye, I saw Arthur draw closer, before his earbud shrieked its complaint and he clapped his hand to his ear, the gaze of the room suddenly upon him. The voice was still listing facts in the same calm tone, mixing with the discordant echoes. Another apology was forming on Arthur's lips, but he was cut off as the middle aged man cleared his throat. Loudly.

"Have some respect. People died." He gestured to the earbuds. "You're all too young to remember." He stepped

197

towards us, and Arthur moved back. "Your father ought to have raised you to give respect where it is earned; take those out."

Arthur's panicked expression faltered, and I saw his eyes narrow slightly. Something flashed across his mind. By the time I figured out what he was thinking, the earbuds were already cupped in his hand. He extended them to the man, who was satisfied for a moment before Arthur's knees buckled and he stumbled into the wall behind him, a plaque clattering against his shoulder and his eyes half rolling back.

There was a sudden burst of motion in the group, the guide freezing in her place and the rest of the group moving back, unsure. The earbuds skidded across the floor, landing near my shoe. I scooped them up, scrambling over to him as the group scattered, backup staff rushing in. By the time I looked over again, the man had slunk away.

I shook Arthur by the shoulders, and he squinted at me, his palm pressed to his forehead. His earbuds were back in a moment later, and I spent a few more minutes convincing the staff that there was no reason to go to the hospital, that there was no cause for an ambulance.

Two free passes and a few minutes later, we were out on the street, and then into a taxi, wind whipping at my hair and silence hanging between us. He spoke first, as the vehicle rose into its route, the city turning from steel giants to a mess of gray lines and glass and steel and buzzing movement.

"I know that wasn't the smartest move."

"No. It was clever, really. You wanted that man to stop talking about you, you got him to stop. Almost everything you do is smart, Arthur. But that was reckless. You could have hit your head on a pedestal or something and cracked your skull open, or you could have never woken up." I didn't actually know I held those fears until I said them out loud. He didn't seem to have thought about it either, looking regretful.

"I know. I just can't stand it when people think they know everything, especially when they don't even try to find out the truth. I was only thinking about how much it frustrates me, and how I knew I could make him regret it, immediately."

"He did immediately regret it. You should have seen his face when you blacked out, he definitely thought he did it somehow. I'm not saying you shouldn't be a little impulsive or immature sometimes, I'm just saying you should remember that I'm here. You aren't just living for yourself. You're not a researcher on a lonely rock, just working for yourself and for the next day. You're living and moving and fighting for Kvir and Ve and the people that have decided to support you, and the ones who have put their freedom in our hands and who have deeply decided that YOU are worth trusting. Think of us before you make another brilliantly terrible choice. "

His eyes were watering slightly, though his face was pressed to the window as he muttered, "I will. Cross my heart."

THE CALL OF
MAN

COM 1

"Among all the tragedies, the sins of human history, the Crisis was, by far, the most easily preventable and the most horribly destructive. We, the people who inherited the Earth, proved definitively that we don't deserve it. And yet, we haven't learned. We won't learn. We should have gone extinct."

[Benji Havahui, A Consideration]

ARTHUR

The museum trip was a little harrowing, but the ride to Nova's apartment was spent in a comfortable silence. I always enjoyed being able to be in a silence that wasn't stifling. Though it wasn't fully silent anymore. The white noise was a constant background, a steady one. It helped my headache ease off again, after the bolt that hit me before my vision had gone dark.

I had faded out of reality by the time we arrived, and only came back into focus as I was climbing out of the car. Nova was pressing a key into my hand.

She was still inside the cab. "I'm going to go see some friends about a way to make your earpiece less noticeable. Let yourself in, and get some rest or something. Rosa gets back from work near the end of the day. Also-" the door closed, and she stuck her head out the window, "Eat something! Have some ginger ale! You'll end up fainting again!"

I nodded, and the taxi was gone a moment later. It faded into nothing, gray disappearing into gray. I wouldn't have admitted it, but my head was still aching, and it felt as if something was jamming into the back of my neck. I moved the key to the lock pad, and it flashed red. Another thing gone wrong. I pressed my forehead to the cool window, but just as I'd half-closed my eyes, the door pushed open and sent me jumping back, blinking my vision into focus so I could properly see the woman who was offering me an apologetic smile.

"My mistake. Most people don't make it a habit to lean on moving doors."

"I'm unique. And my key didn't work."

"Oh? Loiterer or intruder?" There was a slight glint of something in her eyes.

"Guest, but I feel as if I have intruded on some sort of conversation I don't quite understand."

She laughed again. "You're that guy from the news, aren't you?"

I was halfway inside the door, bags in hand, and I honestly considered letting it close behind me as I bolted. I didn't, somehow. Instead, I stood, bracing myself for her comments. There were always comments that followed. People seemed to think that if they knew your opinion, you absolutely *had* to know theirs. During our shopping trip, I had been stopped by two or three people, younger ones, who smiled and muttered "good luck" or "thank you," their voices not holding the boldness of those that felt as if they were worth listening to. I knew that hesitance.

The people who had lots of boldness, unearned boldness, the people who really thought I had to speak to them, that I had to put aside my life to listen to them, they were rarely so kind. They scowled and jammed their accusing fingers into my shoulder, saying "Shame" and "traitor," "fool" and "upstart" and "coward." Nova didn't do much when these people scowled and spat their infuriated words at me, though she seemed itching to spring at them. I didn't hold the defensive anger that she did. I was confused. Utterly blank-minded at the thought that anyone could be so furious at me for trying to save a planet from human destruction. Even more so, how they could be so full of hate at my attempts to free an intelligent species from full-on enslavement. I know now why they hate, though I still can't say I understand.

Thankfully, though the deep lashes of hate outweighed the small notes of support, both were few. I attributed this to the fact that pale boys with dark hair, brown eyes and sweatshirts were as common as clouds. But she had recognized me, and she was one of the soft assurances, sweeping away with a call of "Good on ya! You're a hero." Then she was gone, and I stepped inside with agonizing slowness. It was a moment I would eventually hold close to my heart when I couldn't find the strength to support myself. After she left, I was in a daze. I walked up the stairs, completely forgetting both the fact that the building had elevators and the entire concept of elevators as a whole. No great loss, they aren't our greatest bit of technology. Still, my legs were aching as I reached Nova's door, and the left one was turning in ways it wasn't supposed to, my overcompensation for the limp turning into nails that dug into my back and my knee. The key worked on the door, thankfully, and I pulled it closed behind me as I threw myself onto the couch, shedding the bags along the floor. I planned to clean up, obviously, but at that moment, my bones hurt, and I was just about asleep already.

Neither Nova nor Rosaline had shown up by the time the ache faded, so I stood and peered around the room. The only list item up for that day was getting more public, which seemed complicated and beyond my skills. Also, I had no desire to rush into the public eye or to sweep myself into the whirlpool of attention. Nova would set it up for me. I didn't want to send out a broadcast without her, either. I could have. I could have done lots of things without her, but I didn't want to. I was uneasy, unused to this kind of moment where I had no conflict, no work or task or challenge to overcome. It didn't feel right.

To keep myself busy, I straightened up the kitchen, littered as it was with crumbs and drips and a discarded blazer. I folded the blankets Nova had laid out for me, at least twice, and then, again, I was done. I didn't dare go into their rooms, but I wandered down the short hallway, seeing the pictures on the walls. Pictures were one of the few things still printed, and I skimmed my fingers thoughtfully over the glossy paper, seeing the faces, or places, that were important enough to them to hang up. I wondered how many photos my gallery would consist of.

And as I was sliding back into existential depression amid the mementos, I heard the sounds of motion by the door. It was too early for Rosaline to be off work, so I moved to greet Nova, the door swinging open before I touched it. It was not Nova, as it was, in fact, a man, which Nova was not. As I'd found myself doing, as a habit, I noted three features of his. He was in a suit, black and white, no tie or jacket. His features were sharp. Most distinctly, the left side of his face, below his eyebrow to top of his lip, and his entire left hand, were plated in silver metal, with the eye bright and dangerous red. No way that wasn't on purpose, which made it even more unsettling. My heart began to race.

"Hello, Nova and Rosaline aren't home right now, they'll probably be back soon, if you want to come back?"

Frost was filling my lungs as I spoke, but my face did not betray me.

"I'm here to speak to you, not them."

The frost was solidifying into thick blocks of ice.

He sat down on the couch, which seemed like an odd show of vulnerability, but then it turned out to be more uncomfortable for me, as I found myself forced to move in front of the man, shifting my weight awkwardly from foot to foot as I waited for him to speak. "A lot of people knock and wait. Or use keys, do you have one of those?"

"Some people don't need keys." He overenunciated, just a little. The choice of words pricked at the back of my neck. The way he sat, his tone, they all set me on edge, made me shrink inwards.

"I think that you should leave." The frost was spreading, and I had to push through it to point towards the door." His eyes traveled from my face to my hand, and I felt my fingers curl, shame bringing a bolt of heat across the scar tissue and unnatural bends. I dropped my hand to my side, and he again turned to face me properly.

"I go by Calix. Pleasure."

"My friend is on her way back here, and I really feel like she wouldn't want to come back to a strange man in her, a man she doesn't know in her living room. "

"Ms. Bale? We've met. She didn't mention me? Pity. Either way, this isn't about her. It's about *you*."

The ice had moved up my throat and pushed into my brain. It was spreading, and it burned the back of my skull. I felt it covering bits and pieces. It was going after his name. What was his name. Calix. Calix, Calix. I wished I had my notebook. I blinked, and the ice cracked a little.

"Calix." I had a dozen questions. "So you were here looking for me, not Nova." I wanted him out by the time she got back.

"She doesn't like me much."

I had guessed that was the case.

"And I don't want her involved," he said, suddenly standing. "I want to free you from her."

I was a few steps closer to the wall behind me. Freeing? No. He was wrong. I didn't have to listen to him if he was wrong. "I don't need freeing, so you can go."

Nova. Focusing on Nova pulled the ice inward again, and I felt my fingers unfreeze.

Calix cocked his head to one side, his voice lowering. "You don't? You're just going to let another person make your choices for you? Let another person use you as a face and a name?"

The cold in my chest didn't spread, but it intensified. "She's not doing that."

He ignored me. "I'm here to tell you that you need to stop. There's another way for this to go."

I sighed, somehow comfortable in the familiarity of the protest, and ignoring the twisted concern that laced his words.

"I've heard that kind of opinion from a lot of people, but few force themselves into the room I'm staying in. I admire your tenacity, but please leave." I gestured at the door again, lowering myself into a seat.

"I'm not leaving. I know how much danger you're moving yourself into, I know the rain of arrows aimed at you. The danger, the suffering, why would you risk it?"

I closed my hands into fists. I was suddenly aware of the buzzing of my earbuds, and how they mixed discordantly with his words as he kept talking. "You're scared now, Arthur, aren't you? You've barely started, but you're already tired of the fight and all the danger. Your heart is pounding."

He had risen to his feet and moved closer, by an inch, maybe two. My heart *was* beating fit to break out of my chest. I forced myself to stare at him, directly, forcing my eyes to focus on his. Then, the beating halted, skipping a note.

His eye, the brown one, had a thin screen of blue flashing in front of it. My heart started along its normal rhythm. I rose to my feet, moving in front of the messenger, and then around him. He seemed confused, though I was too determined to take any pleasure in that fact.

"You're not smarter than me, Calix," I called. "You're better connected, but that's all."

I moved into the kitchen, opening a drawer and sliding a paring knife out. It wasn't the sort of blade I was used to working with; those weren't for cooking.

I faced the man, and he stepped back, his hand flicking to his waistband. I looked away, seeing no reason to maintain eye contact as I pushed up my sleeve and slid the tool along the raised part of my shoulder, my skin opening beneath it. I was hit with searing pain, but I gritted my teeth and dropped the tool after the motion was completed. I forced out the health chip and tightened my sleeve around the shallow cut, turning back to Calix. He was at a satisfying and complete loss for words. I held the chip up, between two crimson-dappled fingers.

"You underestimate the pain I've been through. You underestimate my tolerance for suffering. Hear my heart now and see if I'm lying." I was genuine, in the moment, though I can now admire the impact my words had, if only for a second.

Calix, still silent, took a shallow breath. "But why would you want to put yourself through more?" He looked at the device, eyes following it as I sat again, heavily.

"I care about the cause I fight for and the people who fight with me, or that I'm fighting for."

His voice rose for a second, spiking painfully. "Passion is a waste! It leaves you open and vulnerable, and loving people leads to pain and loss!"

I was taken aback, sinking deeper into my chair as the messenger's voice lowered again. His spell had already been shattered.

"I don't hate you, Arthur Keene. I really don't. To hate is still to have passion. I pity you, honestly. I know you're tired, you're aching, and you want to take the world off your shoulders."

My knuckles had gone white, and I suddenly felt cold again, despite the warm blood dripping to my elbow.

"You're going to push yourself until you snap."

I flinched, and that seemed to settle him back into his rhythm. I couldn't speak.

"You don't have to be left without a purpose either, Arthur Keene. You could let me refocus you, guide you into success within the higher powers. You can free your alien pets someday, I'm sure. More importantly, you'll have the life that you deserve. You won't be dragging through strife or exhaustion, or fighting against immeasurable odds." He leaned down slightly, somehow having ended up in front of my chair, and lowered his voice so that I found myself shifting towards him without thinking about it, pulled in. "Put yourself above your silly battles. I was a scared kid too, alone and hurt, and you can improve your life like I did."

Generally, I have trouble looking people in the eyes, but I again pushed myself to meet his gaze. I expected something wild and manic, or something burning quietly— determination or a silent, deep anger. I saw neither, his eyes showing a soul so walled-in that it betrayed absolutely nothing.

"Look inside yourself, and you'll know I'm right." He pulled away and turned, walking out the door and closing it behind him with a soft click and a calm, "Goodbye, Arthur Keene."

I wish I could say I was clever there, that I had a cutting comeback that made Calix limp out with his tail between his legs. But I didn't speak a word. The apartment was nearly silent as I bandaged myself up and changed into one of the new shirts, folding Nova's sweatshirt and laying it carefully on top of the table. The injury wasn't life threatening, and I didn't regret it. I didn't want him to know how I felt, and I didn't want anything from the colony to still be a part of me, nothing physical at least. It made me feel sick. And, after I finished, Nova still wasn't back. I sat on the couch, blank. The people you fight against are supposed to be clearly bad. They're supposed to be angry and screaming or cruel and mocking, supposed to insult and threaten you.

I knew how to deal with the screaming hate and the twisting mocking, but not him. Not that perverse kindness. He wasn't supposed to see me as more than an opposition, he wasn't supposed to know that I was tired and pained. He wasn't supposed to tell me that I should put myself first, or that he didn't even care enough to hate. It was all horribly, horribly wrong, and I didn't know why I was doing it, suddenly. The world was closing in, and I was alone as it did. My head was spinning, and my heart was pounding up into my throat. The world went blurry for a second as I lurched to my bag, taking a gulping breath.

I pulled it open, swallowing dryly as I focused. I saw my notebook, my tablet, my colony jacket, I heard the faint chorus of the city behind my heart pounding, I felt my knees dig into the floor at the edge of the carpet. I tasted blood, but that was something I dismissed. I smelled herbal tea, from the glass broken that morning, and the panic faded, and my world slid back into focus. And I was aware of the gash I had put in my shoulder, and what a terrible idea it was, and I was suddenly sure that I had mostly made terrible choices. But the ones I was sure about, I had made them knowing the battles they would lead to, and I knew that I would fight those battles willingly and stubbornly.

As my heartbeat faded from my ears, I pulled my hands from the bag, and my world settled around me. The walls stopped moving in, cranking away as I forced breath into my lungs.

I hadn't really opened the bag before, not on the ride to Earth, not since we'd ended up at the apartment. Half of its contents were mine, half were miscellaneous items that looked like they had been pulled from storage. I sorted out the rest of my possessions, mainly papers, detailing the projects I didn't want stored digitally, two of the books I'd been rescuing, delicate covers cigar-burned and bunched from being used as coasters or table legs. Neither of them were of any interest to me, and they somehow still smelled like smoke. I kept them anyway. My small, shapeless, child's toy was crumpled at the bottom, legs all askew. I pulled it out and laid it carefully on the shelf, peering at the

213

shadowed bottom as the messenger bag slumped in a pile of canvas. At the bottom laid a scrap of paper, which I pulled out, flipping it over. Liam or the scientist hadn't packed it, it had been there since before the broadcast, when I packed my bag in case I was sent away. It must have gotten stuck when they dumped it out.

It was a small, faded photo of my mother, taken before I was born. My father had brought it when we left, having gotten rid of all his digital ones, and I had found it two years into living at the colony, before things grew really miserable. I still went into his room back then, usually when he was out. I had seen the photo on his desk, and I had taken it and tucked it away under my pillow.

He'd gotten mad, really mad, at everything and everyone, but I didn't give it back. He'd taken every other piece of her away. As soon as she was gone, so was her memory. It was the first little act of rebellion, even though I still sort of thought he was a hero back then. I packed the bag again, pushing it under the coffee table, and placing one notebook painstakingly level on top.

I opened the worn book to a clean page, and I laid the picture flat, smoothing its creases. I hardly needed to look at it, knowing the lines and the colors by heart. She was more full of life, not so paper pale as my father or I, though maybe he wasn't so faded before the colony. I don't think I was. I don't remember. Her hair was darker, too. My father was blonde before the color leached into gray, and mine was yellow-brown still, but not so rich. It used to be sun-bleached, when I was younger. When I played in the green-houses. When I sat with the plants and pressed my face against the glass walls, staring at the richly natural landscape. Her eyes were darker, tilled soil, while my brown was cardboard and dry mud. I wonder, still, what people see when they look at my irises.

After I straightened the picture again, I picked up the bursting book and carried it across the apartment. I took a seat with the tome, sliding onto the floor of the short corridor. I cannot draw, I've never found myself taken with art, as a whole, but I knew anatomy. So, I scribbled a copy of one of the photos of Nova and Rosaline. They didn't look fantastic, but I knew who it was. I put down the drawing and carefully ripped a page detailing a Triller skeleton from earlier in the book, and pasted it in.

That would be my gallery.

I closed the book and packed it without a word. And then, I sat, and remained sitting. And remained sitting.

I remained sitting still as Rosaline arrived back at the apartment. And as she knelt at my side, as she squeezed my hand and checked the back of my head. My sleeve was still down to my elbow, and it showed little evidence of the wound.. Rosaline then left me, my legs bent achingly and the white noise buzzing in my ears as I stared ahead of me, thinking deeply. I heard her moving around in the kitchen, but I didn't look over. I was busy. I wasn't sulking or moping, I wasn't angry or crying. I was thinking. I hadn't been thinking properly. I'd been acting, moving, blank. Not fixing problems, solving things. Fixing problems is what I do best, and it was what I was valued for at the colony.

I was good at it, solving things, and I had a lot of problems at that moment. I needed a list, first, same as the ones

Nova had, but not quite so constructive. Not exactly destructive, but it leaned more toward that sort of idea. People in power have always supported themselves over the needs of the world. Before the crisis, it was those with power that ignored the calling of the masses, and the world was still scarred by their negligence. Cities were uninhabitable from poison rains and the repercussions of fallen power plants. Weather patterns were rarely trackable, and the world was hotter than it should be, the sky hanging heavy with fog and poison.

The world, and those who populate it, still bear the scars of their betrayal. Their silence and their inaction caused a pattern of destruction that has since begun being repeated on other planets, a path of industrialism and ruin left as a proud marker. They knew the past, those that had sent Calix, that had tried to stifle me, and many others.

But, the many knew that. People younger and less powerful but strong in numbers, in each city and on colonies and in ships soaring past a dozen different suns. They had stopped, and they listened.

And that was good.

But it was terrible because I wasn't much of a speaker. I had spoken in public before, spoken from my heart on the broadcasts. But those were planned, written out, or I was too numb and tired to feel the weight they held. When I spoke casually, sharing my thoughts or opinions or my ideas, it didn't always go well. With that said, silence was still not an option. Subservience to oppressive powers was not an option.

I had been, plain as anything, endowed with new purpose, new calling. Not by any divine right, but by the earthbound determination of man. The decree created by those it controlled, from which I could take my words, and my actions, in line with my beliefs.

I knew that I would not only be able to, but be completely willing to devote my life to the cause of others. But first, a moment of selfishness or self preservation. I made my way to the small kitchen, where Rosaline was perched on a seat and thoroughly embedded in whatever was on her screen. I had no desire to be rude, so I folded my hands, fidgeting as I stood in silence.

She looked up after a moment, speaking before I could bring any words from my mind. "Do you need food?" I nodded. "I'll get you something."

"You cook?"

"I work a full time job. Of course I don't cook, I'm fantastic at ordering from the places near my job, though."

I laughed, awkwardly, and accepted the bowl she handed me. She watched thoughtfully as I inhaled half of it. My shoulder stretched as I lifted it, and my breath caught-audibly. She reached out, pushing up my sleeve with light hands.

"Nova's friends couldn't help out, but they know another group that has what you're looking for. You've left an impact on them, it seems. But they're not in the state, so she's staying the night in Michigan, and she'll be back tomorrow." Her fingers prodded slightly as she pulled at the wrapping. "Are you worried?"

I held my breath, dragging my fork around the edge of the dish. "Not at all."

I was nervous, but she knew Nova better than I did. So I focused, spinning the fork between my fingers. I'd learned the trick after seeing one of the temporary botanists showing it off to the others when they were eating. He'd been trying to impress a geologist, I think. I had practiced it for a week or so, but he was at the end of his term at that point, so I didn't show it off to anyone. I still found myself doing it with pens. I can also juggle. That's the end of that.

She got the wrapping off and had moved to clean off the blood that had stopped flowing. I flinched sharply, and the fork went flying, hitting the counter and bouncing onto the floor with a sharp crashing noise. I looked back, almost standing, before Rosaline steadied me. I spoke, in an attempt to ignore the fingers prodding, as lightly as they could, at the open wound near my shoulder. "I'm going to do dinner tomorrow, when you're both here."

"You *can* cook?"

"I can. For one, and not well. It'd be edible. I can do most things, but I was more planning on getting the name of a good place from Nova, and pretending I figured it out on my own."

She laughed, not delicately either, a short burst of joy.

"Well, it's not a deep wound, Arthur"

"I know."

"Of course you do. But that's not the problem. What prompted you to do that?"

I swallowed, my mouth painfully dry. The light mood had faded. "Some messenger, he made me remember the colony chip in my arm. It's not like the little identification ones, it made a little lump in my skin, and I didn't want it to be a part of me. So I got rid of it."

"Cold." She muttered. "It's shallow, not that much blood. Which, of course, doesn't make it okay. Just makes it better.

You won't need stitches, so that's good." she turned away, ducking under the sink.

"Have you ever had stitches? I've got four in my heel from when I fell off a fence and kicked a...."

Her voice trailed off as she stood again, a brown bottle in her hand . I'd pulled off my jacket, reaching back to pull up my shirt. I had stitches. I'd done them with a needle that was literally a shard of stone, and Neolithic-style string made from wood bark, reaching around to my own back.

The scars weren't brave war wounds, they were faded then, an inch across at most, and small, still discolored ridges formed from them. They were heavier on my left side, a cluster above my hip, where my rib had almost poked out. I didn't show that off. It made me sick to think about, which I didn't expect. I suppose I imagined how she'd find my casual relationship with pain. I just didn't want her to think the shallow gash was something that could topple me. I dropped the shirt, pulling my jacket back on over my free arm.

Rosaline didn't say a word. She turned away, but not fast enough that I didn't see her swipe her finger under her eye. I regretted showing her, but what was done was done. I re-wrapped the gash myself and stood, glancing back at the coffee table.

"The sweatshirt. Nova's. Nova's sweatshirt. I got blood, got blood on it. It's over on the table, I don't know how to get blood out." I felt a second of panic, but she moved smoothly over, lifting the garment.

"I can get this out. Nova isn't the only one with siblings. If someone gets hurt, you take care of it, and then hide the evidence. It'll be clean as a clock by morning. Don't worry about that." She patted my hand and hummed as she set the fabric soaking.

"Goodnight, Arthur Keene," she called, moving into her room. I laid on the couch, sort of processing. I rarely dreamed, but that night felt like it could make itself an exception.

COM 2

"When I was younger, I didn't understand what it was to go through a life-altering event. I figured you got upset, you suffered for a few days, and you got over it. I couldn't have imagined the things that'll remind you of what happened, or thinking that you've forgotten it, just to be thrown back onto the moment a month, a year later. "

[Saisen Jessinji, What I Didn't Know]

NOVA

Arthur isn't weak. He wasn't back then, either. However, there are certain aspects of his life that could be, and have been, cited as weaknesses. I couldn't let him be discredited by these exceptions. His scars, his limp, the way his shoulder hung loose. His twitching, his healing fingertips. They'd be fixed, in time, and until that time they'd remind people about all he suffered through. Though I would never tell him to risk his safety or victimize himself by showing them off or keeping them longer than he had decided to, they did serve as something inspiring. For others, at least. To talk about traumas and the like only resonates in the hearts of a few. Major, physical evidence motivates sympathy and support. However, the way he moved, as if to be as small and unnoticeable as possible, or how he couldn't sleep in beds, or how his eyes sometimes shot to the door when he heard loud voices—these things were private. Those were for me and him, alone, to know. The earbuds had already been used as evidence of his nonchalance, and how "casual" his approach to finding justice was.

I'd never call anything about him casual.

Either way, the earbuds I could deal with. It was the issue I'd chosen to solve on that second night back on earth. It was a band-aid on an amputation. It was using casual technology in the place of medical work. I had some friends from college, and some from the foster communities. The one bonus from the childhood that I grew up in. With dozens of kids, low attention, and faced with the traumas of others on the daily, practically from birth. I visited some friends upstate, who sent me to colleagues, who were thrilled to have a part in helping. They worked most of the night, and I stayed to watch, even if I didn't understand most of the engineering discussions.

Uneventful journey, important result.

They'd given me some sort of white noise hearing aid, made for the purpose, at least. Adapted from tinnitus treatments. I was sure Arthur could figure out how to put it in his ear, but I found myself fiddling with the small machine, only tucking it into my bag as I entered the apartment with the first, shaky rays of dawn.

Arthur was curled into himself, his back pressed against the couch and his head resting on his hands to keep his face off of the floor. The room was neat, and no one was passed out over a table, so that was a bonus. I'd gotten some sleep in Connecticut, and some on my way back to the city, and a few cups of caffeine would have to do to make up for the rest. I was halfway through my first mug when Arthur sat up, squinting around the room as he seemed to get his bearings, before he made his way over, a relieved smile forming on his face.

"Morning." He sat down, adjusting his earpieces.

"You're wearing pajamas, what a thrilling display of normal human behavior." I watched him as he rubbed the last bits of sleep out of his eyes

"I just reached into the shopping bag. You may not be thrilled to hear this, but a lot of the clothes I bought look like this. Or jackets and sweaters, I didn't pay a lot of attention, but I love winter clothes. I know the seasons aren't like they were before the Crisis, but we didn't have any in the colony. Tee-shirts too. I like them. And colorful things."

I couldn't help but smile, placing the devices on the table as I went to get my second cup of coffee. He picked one up, squinting quizzically at it. "How does this work?"

"You're the scientist. They didn't give instructions, not that I remember. The inventors send their support, and lead me to have one question. And a follow up question, depending on the answer." He tilted his head quizzically.

"You watched early D.E. movies, correct?"

He nodded. "The bad ones, the good ones, mainly teen ones. Even the realistic ones are wild to me."

I had risen to my feet and was rifling through a drawer in the counter. "You know those classic scenes where they get their ears pierced?" I turned, holding a needle up like a prize.

Arthur paled.

And then he squinted "Sorry, what's that for?"

"Piercing your ear."

"How'd we get from movies to that?"

"That stressful, seriously? Use your notebook. Now sit down over here."

He insisted on reading the instructions a half dozen times, and I took the time to fetch the materials. He needed a helix piercing, for the clasp that held the mechanics and the battery. Worse, he needed another hole pierced through the inside of his ear, which I wasn't sure I could do. But, the hearing aid had to get the white noise directly into his inner ear, without obstructing his outer ear.

I gathered a rarely-used needle, a cork for backing, and a piece of ice. He had raised the ice to his ear, and was staring at the needle as Rosaline walked out from her room, taking in the scene. She joined us at the table, looking curious.

"Why do you look so worried?" She reached across him, grabbing an orange from the fruit bowl. "You sliced your arm open yesterday without a thou-"

I jammed the needle into the table, inhaling deeply. "You sliced your arm open."

It wasn't a question.

"We took care of it," Rosaline protested, as Arthur tugged his sleeve up to show the neat fix.

"The messenger, guy named Calix. He's got a metal face. He showed up, and I ended up pulling out my colony chip. It was pretty cool. But mainly he was just really unsettling. Rosaline says you've met him. It's no major story."

I took another deep breath, picking up the needle again. "I'm taking you with me to work today. Not because of this, but we can talk about it more on our way. And because someone *broke into my apartment* to get to you." I saw him look at the table.

"Not your fault, but it's not safe. Now, hair back and grit your teeth." My tone was calm, if a little clipped. I didn't want to do it, but I couldn't make him, and Rosa hated needles. She grabbed his hand, looking sick. I counted down to two before jamming the needle through, Rosaline groaning at the sight. Arthur was mainly still and silent, his lips tightening against a sharp inhale and his free hand pressed to his temple, clutching his hair. "It gets worse." He looked a little pale, and I wasn't thrilled either. I should have brought him up to Connecticut with me, but it was too late for that. I steadied my hand, noting the right spot of his inner ear. His grip tightened on Rosa's hand, and I jammed the tool through, pulling it out quickly, and throwing it out.

He let go and pulled his hand to his hair, face breaking into a smile. "Classic teenage rebellion. Forget anarchy, a tattoo should settle this. Joke."

I exhaled, finally, and Rosaline managed to drop his hand, grabbing her bag. "I think I'll be early today."

He waved his fingers at her as she slid out of the door, before fixing the earpiece to his ear. It stood out, a little, black and silver, with a thin wire traveling into his ear and clipping into the small pinprick.

The second ear went a lot faster. After, he drifted to the window eyeing the street below before turning back towards me with a bright expression on his face. "I can hear pretty well, and my headache is a lot better too! And while I'm feeling good—" He spun on his heel, facing me again, "I'm going to ask Rosaline to lunch!"

I was taken aback, slightly, a little too tired for any sort of revelation. "I think that would be fantastic." I figured she was kind, she could protect his heart, and I knew he would be genuine and sweet. And they were my two closest friends already. I could get behind that match, though I couldn't figure out who I felt more protective of. "We have about forty minutes before my workday starts, and I'm going to go rest my eyes. Get dressed. The firm I'm working with hired me just for your case, so they obviously want to meet you."

He nodded slightly, and with that, I refilled my mug and strode to my room. The door closed behind me. I took about ten minutes for myself, to think through what I had been told. I didn't think it all through quite well enough, but I had work to prep for and a schedule to keep. So, without nearly enough rest or nearly enough closure, I changed, grabbed my bag, and headed out the door.

Arthur had been sitting against the window, listening to the unobstructed noises of the city as he did something in his notebook. I didn't ask what, mentally preparing myself for our next conversation. We were quiet as we walked downstairs, me keeping an eye on him, and him peering around in fascination. I called a taxi, nudging him over as it pulled up to the curb.

We entered the vehicle in silence, and remained in silence through the quiet groaning of the car as it pulled into traffic. We stayed quiet until the inner workings of the machine had quieted as well. I spoke first.

"So, we've gone through a few topics this morning, and I have moved through a lot of emotions." I didn't face him, scanning the back of the car seat in front of me

"What are you feeling right now?" I saw him glance over, twisting his fingers together

"Hesitant optimism paired with an overwhelming sense of doom." I finally looked over. I couldn't be upset, I was too worried. I'd spent most of my life caring for broken people. Though he was the most shattered, I knew I was his friend, and he was mine, and I was already sure that no amount of bad choices would change that.

He smiled, a little grimly.

"Are you okay, really? And I don't just mean the arm." I was worried, I knew his gash would be fine, but anyone who was willing to rip their arm open was someone that I was worried about. But Arthur nodded, so I pushed the thoughts aside.

"I believe you, so I don't feel bad about this—"

As his features shifted into confusion, I glanced at the driver, who was completely focused on the road ahead of him. Great.

Satisfied, I looked back at Arthur. "That was a terrible, reckless move and you should feel bad about it."

He frowned, bowing his head slightly. It saddened me, that instinct. "Not pulling any punches then, are you?"

I wasn't. I am not a mean person, and I didn't want to be mean to Arthur, but I was full up with worry and anger and overwhelmed and tired, and I wanted to make sure he didn't continue to act so recklessly

"How deep?"

He looked up, matching my slightly clipped tone "Eighth of an inch."

"How wide?"

"Millimeter, maybe one and a half."

"How long, tip to tail."

"Inch and a quarter." The information seemed to make him feel better, and working through it made me feel better too. He had moved his sleeve up, but I had seen the small gash before. That wasn't it. I was just angry that I hadn't been there with him, and I wanted to make up for it.

"Why'd you do it, Arthur?"

"I didn't want the colony chip to be a part of me anymore."

"It was Calix, that snake."

Wasn't a question.

"Yes. He was unsettling. He just knew that I was in pain and I was tired, and he told me to give up, but for myself. He's not the sort of evil I'm used to."

"I know what you mean." I tried to keep up the sternness, but my anger and worry had faded. "Is it discolored? Does it hurt? Is anything wrong?"

"It's a little red, but that's normal. It hurts like a sore arm, not like a stabbing pain, normal. It'll stop hurting in a day and a half. It's clotting right and it's not ripping, which is pretty good." He smiled faintly, looking ahead again.

"And a kitchen knife, Arthur."

"Nearest tool. I'm resourceful. And, I'm not sure if you know this, but your paring knife isn't up to surgical standards."

"I'll note that for the next time."

He opened his mouth to say something, but the vehicle pulled to a stop, and I swiped my finger across the scanner, ducking out of the doorway. He hurried after me, matching my stride as we made our way into one of the city's glass and steel giants.

"And about Rosaline—" I saw his shoulders tense.

"I think you should try it, Arthur." She'd talked to me about wanting to take him out, but I didn't mention that.

The fear dripped out of his stance and was swiftly replaced with eagerness. "Where should we go, then? I would go anywhere, I'd go to a grocery store with her. I find them fascinating, of course, we didn't have nearly that volume or variety or—but what I mean is that I'd go anywhere, as long as she would go with me."

I couldn't help but smile, just a touch.

"But, you think she'd say yes, ye? She's still, ah, interested in males?" I chuckled, nodding "She's perfectly interested in males." It was part of what had made our breakup so unbearable. But I was past it, and so was she, and she was going to be more past it. I was sure she would be thrilled to do something romantic with Arthur. "And perfectly interested in you, I know it. No matter where you go."

He seemed satisfied with my knowledge of Rosaline, and dismissed the subject. I didn't bring up a new one, so we were left in silence, besides the rapidly rising noises of work as we moved through the building. He seemed fascinated, more so than I had been, my first time in the office. I will never stop enjoying his wonder at things I don't see as exceptional. I moved behind him, making sure we found where we were supposed to be.

He stood out sharply among the serious looking professionals. Even I had on my work clothes. But he had no intention of that, not caring about it, and clearly having no inclination to wear the more formal clothes I'd gotten for him. I hadn't looked into his bags, though I'd sort of seen the contents. They suited him, comfortable clothes in all sorts of colors, jeans and tees and jackets and an abundance of pajamas. He liked comfort, clearly, and he deserved it.

He had worn jeans that day, at least, and the oversized work boots that thumped on the floor with each step. Rainbow splattered socks peeked out above the top, but one's gaze was more drawn to his choice of a dark green button down, which was a fine color on him, a fine style, but didn't look good on anyone who chose to leave it open over a yellow belt and a shirt that proudly advertised, in soft purple and aquamarine, with a faint checked pattern, that he was a "Space Cadet" His jacket, which was thankfully slung over his arm, was from the navy and white colony uniform, which really completed the clashing looks with it's ripped off medallions and alien scratched buttons.

No one mentioned his fashion choices as we moved through the various clusters of desks, or the short hallways, or as we moved into the meeting room. As soon as we entered, his shoulders bent again, as he made himself as small as possible when faced with the view of a whole table of people in suits. I saw him force his back straight, though he moved back sharply when the crowd shot to their feet. I slid in front of him casually, giving him a moment to sit as I laughed and spoke lightly with my coworkers. I didn't know any too well, but I knew that they were good people. They all seemed thrilled, too, words piling over each other for a few moments before the room faded into silence.

"So-" I started to speak, before I noticed Arthur opening his mouth to do the same thing. I grew quiet as he cleared his throat, speaking carefully "Hi, I'm Arthur Keene, if you-" He seemed a little thrown off by the applause that followed his statement "if you don't know that. I'm just incredibly grateful to all of you, that you heard the message I was trying to share in my Broadcast, and that you acted." He took a deep breath, leaning his elbows onto the table. "I've been called a lot of things since I landed on this planet. I have been called a lot of rude things, but I've also been called an inspiration and a leader. As nice as that is, if I'm alone, I'm a skinny nineteen year old with half a brain and not much else. I can't change things without support, and you, here, have been the first people to support me."

His words were measured, but genuine. Without a clear end, he lowered himself into the chair, crossing his legs under him before he realized he should sit like the rest of us. There was a few seconds of almost tangible hesitation, before he was again met with a dozen different responses, falling all over each other.

When that faded, I spoke up. "I've told you in my updates, but the mines on Janus are overflowing with horrors, and they show a problem in our society that we, as a group, have put out of our minds. After the Crisis, we spent some time in an idyllic state, making a change in the previous harm done to our world. And then we realized that we didn't need to. Or, we thought we didn't need to. We've spread our industrialization across half the galaxy, and there's missions going further. These aliens, whether living with human intelligence or the brains of a duck, all deserve to have someone defend them. And beyond that. We can't give up this cause that we've found, even planets with only plants and bugs deserve our protection. We're small, but if we stop this, we can make a ripple that will save billions of lives. Cameras don't work in the mines, but we have records of those killed by the cruelty, and Arthur-" I gestured "Knows everything about the oppression." he nodded slightly "More than that, he's someone people recognize, people look to, more than any of the cases you've won and the small changes we've made, this has the potential to be a movement. We need to focus on this, get Arthur into people's minds."

I looked at Arthur, to make sure he was okay. He looked a little green, but his expression was determined. He saw my glance and nodded slightly, and I looked forward again. There were a few moments of muttering before one of the partners spoke up "It'll take some adjusting, but we think you're right. Get us everything you can and we'll look into his public image. I admire your passion, Nova, and yours, Mr. Keene"

"Arthur." His voice was a little high, but steady. "You're helping me do something so great. Please feel free to call me Arthur."

Tight lipped smiles and nods all around, and most of the room rose to its feet. I stayed sitting. Arthur looked over, taking my example. We waited until all but one of the workers had left. With hesitation, I gestured for Arthur to leave. He did, after a short pause. I watched him go, and waited until the door swung shut to turn back to the woman at the other end of the table. She had the power to shut this whole thing down. To cast him out as some sort of deranged activist. She had hired me for his case but I couldn't help but fear that she was regretting that investment. It wasn't like I thought Arthur couldn't handle the possible bad news, but I didn't know if I could.

If we failed, it would be on me. My connections, my job, my contribution. It would be my failure, but it would be worse for him than for me. I was practically holding my breath as she spoke "Do you really think we have the potential to make an actual change?" I nodded, and she continued, thoughtful "We're a business, still. We can't put all our energy on this. We will be able to get someone to help out with his public image, and we'll share whatever information and other resources we can, but you'll have to handle it."

I nodded, unable to keep a relieved smile off my face. "Thank you, we can change the future of humanity."

As we stood, she quipped "The time for speeches is over, Ms. Bale. I expect action." I was out the door, already searching for Arthur, for a moment, before I spotted him. He had a deer-in headlights look in his eyes, and had backed up almost to the wall behind him. I stayed hidden behind the door, but moved enough to see who he was shrinking away from. It was a man that I knew better than some. He wasn't quite a good person. Not evil, per se, just low level annoying. He never stopped talking about what schools he went to, all the experiences he had. He didn't like me, because I was younger than him, and I had chosen to quit the job he dreamed about now. He was heavily bought in with the aristocracy inside the government, and enjoyed gossiping about how he was going to join the ranks of the rich.

He wasn't a big fan of people with morals.

So it made sense that he was the one that had put such panic onto Arthur's face. I almost moved to confront him, but instead, waited. This could be my opportunity to get him fired, and then he wouldn't mess with people like that anymore. Anyway, Arthur would hate to have me jumping after him instead of having any faith. I listened as closely as I could, crooking my neck to catch the words he hissed out from between his teeth.

"You're an insolent, entitled, traitor."

It must have been an unpleasant adjustment, getting mad at someone that looked like him.

"*If* you even get your 'movement' going, it'll fail before anything gets done. It won't get out of this tiny, pointless little stepping stone. Listen to someone older than you, smarter than you. It won't even get out of here, I'll make sure of that."

He had prodded his finger into Arthur's chest, and at that, I jumped out from behind the door. I grabbed him by the arm, shoving him away. "Back off, Anderson. And, after that, I'd get your two week notice in. It'd be better to retreat back to your trust fund than to get fired from a stepping stone like this place." He looked about to burst, before his face whitened as the woman stepped out of the office behind me. I tilted my head, smiling with my favorite kind of passive aggressive politeness. Arthur noted the situation, a dawning realization growing in his eyes, and pulling up a small smile with it.

We left, fast, and I waved down a taxi, not having time to wait to call a car or the desire to make Arthur walk. On my own, I'd take the train. I started chuckling as the car pulled up, and he began doing the same. We laughed loudly as we entered the car. I dropped my face into my hands, and he wiped tears of mirth from his eyes. "His face," I coughed out

"And I thought that I was spiteful" Arthur looked at me, joyful.

"No. You're reckless when your morals are challenged, *I'm* spiteful. He deserved to be fired, anyway. He's been harassing everyone in the office since before I got there, and he's from a wealthy family, got good schooling, he'll find another place to be insufferable." Arthur's enthusiasm seemed dampened, but it was the truth. We were in a rare happy moment, though, so I changed the subject. "Rosaline started work a couple hours ago, so I'll tell her to take an early lunch break and I'll leave you by the office. You can ride home after on your own, and I can send all the records to the firm."

He shook his head "No, you've done far too much work."

"This isn't work. You spent months making these records, and then three weeks organizing and translating and memorizing them. This is a two minute message, five minutes putting you on social media, and then both of my room-mates are out of the house for an hour and I can take a nap." He nodded, slowly. I couldn't wait to go home and collapse onto my bed. I loved Arthur and I loved Rosaline, but I also loved sleep. And, though I didn't absolutely love it, I had to field calls from a half dozen relatives about why I was on the news, how I met Arthur, what I thought I was doing. But the time zones were different enough that I could procrasti-nate an hour longer.

"I think you might be my best friend, Nova. I haven't had one of those in a while" He wasn't looking at me, scarred finger picking and twisting at a loose thread in his seat belt.

"Thanks, Arthur. I've had a couple, but none quite like you" Rosaline, I would've said, was my best friend, but she'd become more like…something I couldn't name at that moment. I'd dated her, and I couldn't feel like that about him, but I'd known her longer, but he was just kind, and magnetic, and it felt like a chosen friendship. Not friendship you make because you're put next to someone in class. I chose to go to him, and he chose to follow me back.

The cab stopped in the middle of a few blocks of soaring buildings. Not the artistic ones, either, with their mirrors and swirls and balconies. They were stiff and tall and built unnaturally high, from back when they started running out of room on the planet. Arthur slid out the door, and I sent a message to Rosaline. I waited, in the cab, staring at his back as he shifted uncomfortably. He had, thankfully, left his jacket with me, but he still didn't quite fit in.

It looked almost picturesque, the scene through the win-dow. He was facing away, but I still caught the aquamarine and the purple from his shirt as he fiddled with the button down. He was painfully still, too. He had no intent. Nowhere he was rushing to. He looked around, and I caught the expression on his side profile, before I saw his face light up. It was incredible. The city was shrouded in dusty gray fog, but he seemed to glow as he started to step towards Rosaline, who was speed walking over to him, her steps reserved but clearly hiding that she wanted to rush over. He wiggled his fingers in an uncomfortable greeting, before dropping his arm to catch her hand. She lit up then, as well, and I turned away, the cab carrying me home.

COM 3

"Being teen-aged is suffering. Not all the time, and not for everyone. But at their core, these years are full of people just a little bit miserable and trying to find things to make themselves feel a little better. They're full of people who are angry, too. And rightfully so. The teenage breath hangs heavy with angst and frustration and an overwhelming feeling of injustice."

[Julio Jameson, It's Awful]

ARTHUR

There's not much to say about the date. Actually, there are some things, I'm sure, that could be said, but there isn't much to say. Nothing that I can think of, at least. I took her hand first, but she pulled me along. She seemed all serious before I touched her, looking just like the other grains of sand falling through the hourglass. She burst into color when she began guiding me, a little too fast, but I just stiffened my leg and ignored my limp. We got something to eat and then she said we absolutely *had* to go to eat it on top of a skyscraper. I *had* to see the view. So, we did. The height was startling compared to the land I was used to, but I looked into the sky and reminded myself that I'd been there. Then, she helped me grab a cab, and she kissed my cheek before disappearing back into the grains of sand. I told the driver Nova's address, and then, I was back. I went through the records, working on a speech.

The room was silent for a while, aside from my muttering, my testing whether a word fit or not, if a phrase was right or wrong. It rarely felt right. I didn't quite feel right, either. But I worked, because that was what I could do. I should do. I did. I worked and muttered until Nova emerged from her room, phone to her ear and shouting in an odd language mix. Languages were confusing to me, on Earth. Evolved English was universal, technically. Everyone knew it. It was spread in the name of unity amid whispers of superiority. But there were heritage languages as well. With a lack of translation, regional languages stewed together. Evolved Scandinavian, European, Australian. Continental or regional Asian and South American tongues. That was easy enough, I'd learned what I could from dictionaries and study guides. Not enough to pass; all my knowledge was Pre-Crisis, when things were distinct and had neat language rules. And slang, didn't like that. The slang in each language, the dialects of evolved English all grew from nationalism and cultural pride.

Again, I was forced to yank myself out of my own thoughts, as Nova sat on the seat across from me. I realized she'd ended the call and turned to speak with me.

"-Go?" I looked confused, I figured, because she repeated her question. "How'd it go?"

I nodded.

That was *not* the right move, of course, as she furrowed her brow in matching confusion. We stared at each other for twenty seconds or so before my processors all got working again.

"It went well. Nothing much to say."

"How'd the hearing aids work?" She gestured.

"I could hear, yeah, though I've still got a sort of ringing in my ears. My headache has faded, so overall good, all good."

Her brow was still furrowed, but she nodded anyway. "Glad to hear that. I think you two are good for each other."

I hoped that she was right, and it seemed like all the facts were pointing towards her being right. Rosaline was kind and challenging, and she wouldn't hurt me or make things difficult, and that felt right. Though, what did I know about what was supposed to feel right? I'd never felt quite like people should. I thought it was normal, but I knew consciously, in that moment, that it couldn't be right. It was fine though, at that moment. Because, in that moment, I figured I could move past everything and find my sense of normalcy. I had time, had freedom, had support, and romance, then.

At that moment, the romance walked through the door, throwing herself on the couch next to Nova. Rosaline looked up at me, and I swore I saw some of that wrongness flash in her eyes, before she smiled and turned away, facing Nova instead.

"It's Nova's turn to get dinner, and it doesn't look like she's done that," she noted, and Nova tugged a pillow over her eyes, grumbling. I moved to volunteer, but Nova was already on her feet.

"Arthur, you will be added to the calendar, but let me grab it tonight." I sat back again, watching her scoop up her jacket and move to the door. She glanced back at me with a knowing grin and a lightning-fast wink. I didn't know what she meant with those expressions, but she was out the door before I could ask. I wouldn't, anyway. Not with Rosaline in the room. She thought I was sort of cool.

Now, she was wrong about that, but I planned to keep up my illusion of social adeptness, at least until I got to know her as well as I knew Nova.

Nova had thought I was cool at some point before she met me. She had said so, and I had told her she was wrong. She believed me within a few days of getting to know me.

I looked at Rosaline again, and she was looking at me. Her features were held in a small smile before they suddenly burst into a full-on grin. Like Nova had before she left, more joyful but just as carefully curated. She jumped, really jumped, to her feet, and grabbed her bag from where it had been dropped, on the carpet next to the door. She'd left the door open, just a half inch. I noticed that in my normal flashes of observation.

I didn't do anything about it. I made myself focus on Rosaline. She had the bag open on the table, and was digging through it. It had been organized, it looked like, but she'd begun rushing and had messed most things up. That bothered me, but I again dismissed that. It wasn't an issue worth a conversation. I leaned over the table slightly, suddenly intrigued by the papers that she sifted through. I had reached out for a file folder, almost taking it in my hand, before she pulled out the papers she'd been searching for, a flourish in her gestures. Something about that unsettled me, but nothing I could put my finger on. I looked at the papers, but she had pulled them back and flipped through them to the last page. There were only a few lines of text on the last page. But it was paper printed, so it had to be important.

Rosaline explained, "It's the lease we got when we started renting the apartment. We're not supposed to have three people, but an exception was made because our landlord's a fan. I want to make things official. I want to make you officially one of us, part of this little family. Also, a more proper resident of Earth. I figured it might help with the transition, you know?"

She smiled, again. This one was small, more hesitant, and it hid a thousand words that I couldn't quite make out. My heart almost burst, and I fell over myself to find a pen, digging one out of my messenger bag and tipping the whole thing over in the process. I'd clean it up later, I figured. I lived there, so I had to. It was fast, too fast to move through the dozen emotions I felt crawling at the edge of my consciousness. I pushed them back without sorting them.

I had plenty of time; this was a moment of permanence. It lasted longer than most moments did, just pausing before it lazily dripped away with the sound of my pen scratching my name into the paper. I didn't have a signature, so I just let the letters run together, a mess of shapes that meant that I had a place. A small niche in the world, in these people's lives. I teared up again.

Rosaline hugged me. Her embrace was a little tight, almost desperate. I took what comfort I could from it, and sat back, laughing sharply. She gathered the papers and packed them again, the smile held on her face. It was altogether a lot of smiling. She glanced at her screen, excusing herself to check some message or something. I stared at my pen for a few seconds, thinking about what it had done. I placed it in my bag with a sort of reverence, leaving it as I began cleaning up the papers. I had moved over by the door to gather up some particularly adventurous notes. Right then, the door slid open, and I looked up with Nova's name on my tongue, my eyes ready to meet hers.

It wasn't her. My eyes met two others, though. A dark one, almost black, and a red one. He wasn't alone this time, wasn't creeping or charming. There were a half dozen soldiers behind him. One of them grabbed my arm and tugged me to my feet. She was taller than me by an inch, maybe. She had dark hair. It was in tight curls and pulled back on the nape of her neck. The papers hit the floor and were crushed under seven pairs of feet. I spoke then, crying out for the sake of my papers, not myself. Rosaline was looking out from behind the wall around the small hallway. Calix tipped some sort of imaginary cap to her, and my heart sunk. He turned to me, then, clicking his tongue sympathetically.

"I gave you a chance, Arthur Keene. Now, I'm afraid, you're under arrest for treason and attempted incitement of violent revolution. And all that's only made worse by you illegally entering the planet." Somehow, the one to his left had gotten the short stack of papers, and he half gestured to the signature marks "and you admitted it to, incredible."

I opened my mouth to release my vain protests, feeling the stammer rise deep in my chest. I couldn't have gotten a word out, even if Calix hadn't brought his mechanical hand onto the base of my neck.

There was a short crackle, and a shock pushed to the edge of consciousness. Nova had shoved through the small crowd by then, and they made no efforts to stop her. The bag she was carrying hit the floor, and she almost lunged at Calix. Rosaline grabbed her and pulled her back. Then, my eyes focused on the bag again, which had begun to fall in slow motion as it tipped onto the carpet. I didn't get to see its contents, because the world, again, went black.

That had never been a good thing for me.

THE CALL OF
ADVENTURE

COA 1

NOVA

I don't want to say it, or think it, even. Still. But it has to be said, and I've got the practice of thinking it a hundred times or more. And better I say it than Arthur. He's said it, though, the words tainting the air with salt. He's thought it too, I know, maybe more than I have.

Rosaline betrayed us.

After Arthur's eyes had closed into a mask of sick peace, they pulled him out the door. I didn't see any of the soldiers' features, preferring to leave them faceless. But Calix, I saw. I would have hit him as soon as I saw him if Rosa's fingers hadn't dug into my forearm. He stopped thoughtfully, seeming to consider his words for a moment. The silence hung throughout the room, thick and dark and on the edge of exploding. I pulled my arm free, harshly, and stood just a step away from him. My hands were held in fists at my side.

"Those papers. They're nothing."

"Fair, but they're also enough. We both know it."

He was right, though I wouldn't say it then. Instead, I bit my cheek and pointed at the door. If he stayed a moment longer, I knew I would grab things and start throwing.

"Get out. I know you've got some clever jab or quip or something, But don't. Just get out of my home."

His face twisted, and he looked almost hurt, but stalked out behind those goons, pulling the door closed with a painfully loud click. The door bounced back open with the force, and Rosaline walked over to shut it, refusing to face me.

"Rosaline, I need you to look at me."

She did.

"What happened?"

"My life would have been ruined, Nova. Yours too. They said so."

"Rosaline."

"They told me to have him sign the fake confession, get the fingerprint, and record the whole thing to verify it. So I did—I had to. We've worked our whole lives, and I can't throw that away, like you did. We've been working so long for this."

I'd never been more hurt.

"For this??! We didn't work for money or for prestige. We've been working to change the world, and you just got our chance sent to jail. And more than that, he's a kid. An innocent nineteen year-old kid. He hasn't done anything wrong, and you know it. I don't care what they told you, that he's dangerous or anarchist or whatever. He doesn't deserve that sort of betrayal."

The words were ripping from my throat, and I was shouting, almost, but I forced my tone deathly civil.

"He didn't even do anything wrong, there wasn't anything for him to confess."

"That doesn't matter, you know that."

"He wouldn't sign anything like that."

"I told him that I wanted to sign him onto our lease here."

My heart collapsed inwards like a dying star. It felt like she had punched me and I wanted to hit her, to shout at her again. I collected myself, forced calm, and faked it until It sunk in.

"Rosaline. You made him think he had a home, when you were taking any chance he had at a semi-normal life away from him. When you were young, you didn't have a home, I thought you'd know."

Her voice spiked as I rose to my feet. She matched me, her hands out defensively. "Nova, Nova, look. I couldn't ruin my life over him. He'll be fine, you know he will. He'll only be there for a week, if that, and they won't hurt him!"

"He'll be there as long as they hold him before he goes to court, and they're good at drawing that out. You've made everything a lot worse. Did you bother to know anything about him? He's injured! He has these headaches and that limp.. And he's anxious, and he's going to get hurt!"

I was angry, angrier than I had ever been. Especially at her. We hadn't fought, really fought- since eighth grade.

We'd started arguing about something that didn't matter, and I ran out of her house with frustrated tears on my skin. Two days later, some boys in class stepped on the back of her shoes until they fell off, and I walked next to her to help kick back at them, and we moved on.

"You're *supposed* to be the person that doesn't hurt me. We promised. And you saw everything that I went through to get Arthur here" My voice kept going up, I couldn't stop it. "This isn't business or politics. You saw me come home from a dozen interviews, you know how much this matters to me." My throat felt raw. "And he'll be out soon, fine. I know. I know that because I'm going to go fix the good thing that you just absolutely destroyed."

I was in front of the door now, and it was still open. "I'll send friends to come and get my things. I just..." I paused "We promised. We promised not to hurt each other, and this hurts so much." I pulled the door open and fell back against it. My chest was flaming as the star tore at my insides, burning every bit of me. It flared into my throat and seared for a moment before suddenly turning to nothing. My legs were too hollow to let me stand and my chest was about to cave in so I sat against the door and let the handle press painfully against my ear. Whatever had pushed me through that argument was gone, and it ached somewhere deep down.

COA 2

"Everyone's life has a worst moment. Even the sheltered people. It's a fact. Even if everything is great, there is still a moment worse than the others..Then, on the other side; Even if your world is full of terror and suffering, there will always be a moment that stands out as the Worst."

[Enlin Diayed, Scars]

ARTHUR

My eyes opened slowly, with far more effort than being awake is worth. For one horrible moment, as white walls and blinding fluorescence assaulted my view, I was caught in a sickening, overwhelming wave of fear. I should have known it. I should have known it. It was all I could think. I must have hit the ground and they'd dug me out and brought me back to my room. No one cared about what I said, there was no movement for freedom, there was no Nova Bale, no New York apartment, no Triller children that listened as intently as I fumbled through a story in their language. It was all just my synapses firing randomly. There was nothing.

I realized, suddenly, that I had closed my eyes and was holding my breath in my lungs. I had to stop that, though I didn't see much reason why. So I opened them again. My breath came short and shallow. The air tasted recycled, and I grew steadily more despairing. I was dazed, but demanded my vision clear, and so it did, revealing a room that opened up far larger than mine in the colony. I then realized that I was not, in fact, laying down, finding myself propped up against a plain wall. My hands were folded in my lap. I wiggled my fingers. Nothing seemed broken, no bones cracked or poking out of my chest. There was no skin ripped open or scraped down to the red. I rolled my shoulders, ache rising and falling, but without the normal stabbing pain. I looked down again. My shirt was blue and purple, with the words across my chest. I didn't have shirts like that at the colony. And, as I looked around the room, it didn't quite look like mine did. No bed, much larger, half filled with lab equipment. Didn't look like the colony labs, though. It wasn't arranged right. Can't believe I noticed this last, but there was someone working at one of the tables. He looked younger than me by a year, or by five, couldn't tell. I considered that I was having one of those younger self hallucinations. But, alas, no. His hair was darker than mine was, and his eyes were lighter. I couldn't tell the exact color, but his gaze was more intense than almost any I'd seen.

"Hey!"

I shouted at him, trying to catch his attention. He didn't look up. So, I waved my hands in the air, still feeling too unsteady to stand. He kept his focus on his work, though his gaze twitched to me, for just a second. I scowled, spite over-ruling confusion. Objectively? That's a bad thing. But to me, at the moment, it was a blessing. I dragged myself to my feet, too, feeling low pain and just a little unsteadiness. I made my way all the way over to the table. It was light-weight steel, not stainless, and cold under my hands. I reached out towards a beaker, and the boy finally looked at me. He had green eyes, and they were glaring "Don't touch that."

"What?"

"You'll throw it off." I swear he glanced at his hand, before looking up at me "give it a minute."

I didn't have the time to ask for more details before the door across the room hissed open. Another figure. This one was hooded, and moved with slow, planned steps. Its feet dragged, just a little. I looked at the scientist, who made no move to back away. And then, back at the Hood.

His face was, notably, near featureless, with one exception. His eyes, shifting between a spectrum of pale colors, showed expression, anticipation, manic joy, anger, even. In contrast, the boy seemed far more dangerous in his silent, neutral observation, unmarred by those same human traits. Confusion pushed against fear, and nausea twisted with both.

I was right about the danger, it seemed, as I looked back over in time to see them lunge at each other. It felt like some fever dream, hand connecting with nose, heel with stomach, with knee, body with floor. The young one, who scrambled back to about a foot away from where I stood, on the other side of the table. I was frozen, but that didn't affect them. He managed to catch the rounded edge of one of the metal chairs, and sent it flying. It hit the man and then the floor with a pained groan and a clatter, respectively.

It fell to pieces, and both were on their feet with a short metal pole in their hand, breathing heavily. In a whirl of motion, the boy ducked and hit him in the stomach, and the hooded man was down. One of the boy's loafers was on his wrist. He swung the metal pole, and I heard it hit flesh. He tossed it aside and looked over to me, head cocked. "Blink," he ordered.

I felt my stomach twist around itself, but slowly blinked. As my eyes opened again, there was a loud ringing in my ears-louder ringing, and the body, the glass, and all of the lab equipment began disappearing. He sighed, tugging off the small dots that had begun to appear on his face as he walked back. I drew back against the wall as the younger man approached.

"You need to take those off."

He pointed, and I brought my shaking hands to my face. Small circles were raised above my skin, and I pulled them off.

"What was that?"

"Simulation. If it's your first run through the ending one is a basic program, and the most basic sim is a combat sim. Get them down, it ends."

My confusion was visible, clearly, as he spoke again, with a long suffering exhale through his teeth. "My name is Renn Hawthorne. You got arrested, but you're not in a prison yet because they need some information first. This room is meant to create an illusion in your head, little dots are noting your brain activity during that.—" he gestured around the room, which was still stark white and plain, but smaller than it had been before. The smooth plastic walls were now textured, and the room was empty aside from two metal cases embedded in the walls, and a metal panel in the floor. Having assessed the room, I took stock of myself, letting Renn's voice fade into the background as he finished explaining the surroundings. My clothes looked as they should, and my earpieces were planted in my ears, though I had a buzzing headache and an aching pain like they had been yanked out and jabbed crudely back in. There was a red mark on my neck; it looked a little scorched.

I remembered the taser and found myself wincing, though it didn't burn at that moment. I could have guessed that would be there, but there were pinpricks and friction marks down the front of my forearm. I dismissed my worry, because if I didn't, I wouldn't have been able to think.

I brought my thoughts back onto him, as he finished his sentence. "That was a simulation. We have gone through ten together, and you went through five before that.

You're probably a little out of it, and you may be a little sore."

"I'm Arthur, Keene Arthur. Arthur K-"

"Arthur Keene, I know. Keep going, I know you have questions and I need to finish this up"

I shrugged, brushing off his curtness. "You're angry, aren't you?"

"Angry within my right."

"How do you know about the simulations, how do you know how many there were, why don't I remember the first fourteen, and why do I remember the last one?" I massaged my temple, trying to put myself together.

He sat in front of me as I slid down the wall, taking a moment to consider. I saw that his eyes were green, and he was wearing a school uniform-looking getup, with the union crest on the pocket.

"I know because I have experience and access to enough information to be able to tell. Again, I have experience. I have tricks and strategies. Plus, my brain works differently than most people. I know they're finished because they do it in tens and fives. You remember the last one because it is simple, short, and it makes you unable to trust me. Not that I want you to, I don't trust you." He gestured passively at the place where the body had fallen, now just a section of clean, white floor.

I was a little offended, admittedly, but his suspicion was probably justified, so I moved on, because I had a lot more questions.

"Were the others longer? Or more complex? Did the room look the same? Why would I be sore if it's a simulation? What are some tricks you know? Why do you have so much experience? How do I get out of here? Why are you here, why am I here, and why are we together? Also, if you have access to the files, are you not a prisoner? And why'd you sit and answer my questions?"

I liked knowing things, exchanging information. Renn looked like he regretted deciding to talk to me. Still, he answered.

First though, he pressed his fingers together, watching them with a drawn brow. A moment of silence, and then he looked back at me, seemingly satisfied with whatever it was he'd seen.

"Some of the others were longer. Time works differently in a simulation. It can be drawn out, stretched, and go on forever." He looked serious. "They were more complex, sure, and they looked different. Different rooms or outside or in cities or other planets. You'd be hurt because you don't get physically injured, but your pain receptors can be thrown all out of whack. I once woke up with stabbing pains everywhere below my waist, and another time I got out with my hand looking like a bag of bones because I'd hit a wall and I didn't realize it in the simulation. I have a lot of experience because I've been in and out of these since I was a child. I was born into this. I'm not telling you my strategies because I'm not yet sure that you won't hand them back to-" he again gestured passively around "and I'm-'

I began to protest, but he seemed hurt, and deeply so, too deeply for my words to bypass.

"I'm here because I was born to be here, basically. And since I've been doing it my entire life, I've been broken down time and time again. They know my brain, they want to know yours. I'm not a prisoner, technically. I *have* been out a couple times, but it's always with a dozen people a foot away because they know I'll run." He raised his voice slightly, eyeing a corner of the ceiling. "And you know I'll be able to disappear." He looked back at me, "They don't care. Anyway, I'm talking to you because you're the first person here in a while that *may* not work for them. I've thought that before, though. Either way, nothing I'm telling you is intimate or secret, and they know it already."

He paused, sighing again "In the simulations, when I was unprepared, you moved to help me first. If you knew in advance that you were going to be there, you wouldn't have gone through that pain. People aren't like that."

It sounded ridiculous, outlandish, too much. Honestly, just a wild story. But he spoke matter-of-factly, he moved like he was ready to fight, and he looked wise and deeply aware of his suffering, how it was his reality.

"Like I said, They know how I work, Arthur, but not you. That makes you dangerous. As dangerous as me? Generally, no. You're clearly not a fighter, even if your strategic instincts are better than some. They'll probably send you to prison soon. Or not. Maybe you'll go back to your Union job. It won't be of any consequence to me." He moved back, shrugging casually. My heart broke for him, just a little.

My sympathy shifted into self-pity soon after, as I pushed off, and half of my muscles groaned in protest.

"Oh, sit down," he called behind, annoyed by my making him pause by the wall. "I'll see you in the news then, I suppose, unless you're stuck in prison. You'll probably be stuck in prison, though."

"I have a lawyer."

Nova would help me, definitely. I didn't do anything wrong, and she knew that.

"Ms. Bale. She isn't a criminal lawyer."

"I'm not a criminal."

"Not a tree, either, are you?"

I frowned, growing a little doubtful. She would help me, though, she could. She was smart. And she couldn't have been working against me.

"Whatever happens," I had, at some point, dropped down again, but I pointed at him from the floor "I won't be as defeatist as you."

At that, he spun, eyes narrowed angrily. "Defeatist? You really aren't even smart enough to be with them. And if you're not, you'll be fine, but know that if I allowed myself the luxury of not fighting back" His voice dropped a little quieter, and his hands were still at his sides "-of even an hour of selfish defeat, I wouldn't be here. I would be out there, killing and fighting and destroying because that's what a weapon does. You got tased? Once? So what! Move past it. You're going to prison? Whatever. I know you'll be out before long. So what you have to do is; get through it, get out, and make some change. You're a public figure and your friend is smart. Now, I'm going to have to go into a pain-filled simulation that teaches soldiers how to kill people. Try not to drown in your self pity."

The wall opened into a plain doorway, and two of three people in uniform slid in, surrounding the boy. They swept him out of the room, and he was gone in seconds. A few more stepped in, I felt a pinprick in my arm, and my eyes closed.

COA 3

NOVA

I was working like mad.

I had absolutely no time to waste. If they were willing to bring him to trial, it would be corrupted. It was more likely they wouldn't, but that was hardly better. They'd sweep him away, make sure he was forgotten, wait until his support faded, until people stopped believing that he was going to change the path of the world

But he could, and I knew it. I had let my life fall to pieces around the *chance* that we could bring a change into the universe in which we dwelt.

So I stayed closed off and exhausted, alone, and honestly a little terrified, for that small glimmer of a chance that my actions could be of some consequence. For that, I worked.

For that, I persevered against an opposing force whose powers I was just beginning to see.

For that, and for Arthur Keene. Probably my best friend at that point, but it wasn't all that selfish.

COA 4

ARTHUR

I woke up in another unfamiliar room. Another cursed secondary location. It was starting to become a habit, getting knocked out and waking up in some mysterious setting. Frustrating. But, if I think hard, also a little ego-boosting. What damage was I believed to be able to do, when conscious? Unfortunately, cons outweigh pros. By a lot. I had an absolutely beating headache from the sedative.

Or, maybe not from that. I brought my hands to my head, noting a distinct lack of ear pieces. The room was silent, too. I blinked the world into focus, scrambling over to the nearest wall without yet being able to drag myself to my feet. I scanned the area, the cell. It was dull, with grayish walls and a heavy door, closed, of course. There was a small, closed off bathroom by the door. It looked a little like my room in the colony. A bit darker, no windows, and no desk spilling over with neat stacks of books and papers.

There was a low cot, and I crumpled onto it, glancing downwards at my plain clothing, white and navy. The union symbol was embroidered neatly on the pocket of the slacks, and neat, blocky numbers ran down the arm. It made me feel sick. I looked around the room again, but it was plain, dull, and it was completely

Utterly

Silent.

The walls began to close in as waves of fear and nausea rolled over me. My breathing sped up, and I couldn't move, not an inch. My pounding heart and the buzzing in my ears created a background melody as my eyes rolled back in my head.

I blacked out once again more before I pulled myself together enough to stay alert. It hurt, and the ground looked inviting, and my lungs and stomach twisted together inside my throat. But my fear had passed and my head had cleared a little, and I made efforts to push through it.

"Hello?"

I called, and then again. Twice more. Not a word in response, but I heard footsteps shuffling outside.

"I know there's someone out there." I knocked on the wall and immediately felt my knuckle split against the rough surface, yanking my hand back to my chest.

I paced in silence for a moment before starting to speak again. Not to the person outside, but to the walls and to the air and just to fill the room with noise. I recited the alphabet in every language I knew, counted to a thousand, and then skipped around to ten thousand. The family names and genus of every animal I could think of. Quotes and excerpts, until my mouth grew dry and my voice was gone. That was when I slept, technically. I didn't eat much either, though I measured time by when the plain plates were nudged through the door. That was how I knew it had been two days before someone else spoke.

I had moved past names and citations and facts. I had started, instead, talking out what I was doing, why I was pushing forward, everything I'd been doing. And speeches. Speeches too. Repeating old ones and planning new ones. I was trying to remember the word "unconstitutional" when I finally heard someone else.

"*What* are you doing??!"

The words burst forth in a cloud of static. That, in itself, was incredibly odd. I later found out that they used early digital-era technology because modern tech was believed to be able to be turned into a weapon for escape. Renn could've probably got out with a speaker and a button.

But I digress. I faced the wall, picking the shiny gray of the device out from the dull gray of the wall so I could talk directly to the source of the voice.

"I'm talking, making noise." I threw my arms up in a tired gesture.

"You are aware that people don't actually get let out of prison by annoying the guards."

"It's not for you. Silence gives me headaches."

The voice probably already knew, though it hesitated for a moment before a very soft "Oh" sounded from the speakers.

"Yeah." I called, dryly. "Happens when you fall down a mine."

"I know, I read the news." The voice sounded a little defensive. "Also heard it when you were..dictating your memoir."

"I wasn't dictating my memoir. I was trying to figure out why I'm still doing this. With the odds all stacked against me, I'm not sure why I'm going on." I dropped down again, listening to the static.

"You didn't actually sound unsure, not for a second."

"You are, unfortunately, correct." I wished I'd been able to hesitate and at least consider stopping, being safe and comfortable, but that wasn't going to happen.

"I've got to stop talking." The words were a bit clearer, and I heard some sort of genuine thoughtfulness behind them.

"I figured. But, I don't have to do any such thing. Just, before you stop, give me a name. I don't want to just talk to the walls." I listened hopefully.

A crackle of hesitation, and then, "El."

I nodded to myself, satisfied, as the speaker turned off. And from that moment on, I spoke still, though with a face in mind. El, to me, was an Eleanor. A bright eyed brown haired twenty-something. I hadn't met a lot of Els, and the static obscured any sort of clues to what they looked like. In my head, I only saw shapeless features, but I didn't need a clear look. I just needed someone to talk to, or at. El spoke sometimes, but more often communicated their presence through a quiet crackling, a small relief.

Two more days passed after we first spoke, and I stopped talking. I just stopped. My voice trailed off, my words ran thin, and I lay on the ground, my eyes tracking patterns in the pots of light that flickered across my vision. I stayed like this, had to. The room faded into the background, its ringing a chorus of anvils clashing in my mind. I lay perfectly motionless, as a wheedling voice joined the chorus.

"Aren't you tired, Arthur Keene?"

I almost nodded to the voice. I was tired. Really tired. My body dissolved into millions of particles, and they floated through the air and the air vents and around into the world outside where I deeply, horribly wanted to be. My particles yanked themselves sharply back together as the speakers crackled to life.

"Arthur."

I sat up. "What?"

"They say you haven't been talking." I couldn't pick up any kind of tone amid the static.

"I haven't."

"Doesn't that give you headaches?"

"Yeah. Blinding ones." I threw my hand over my eyes as if to illustrate the point.

"Then why aren't you talking?"

"I don't have anything to say, I suppose." There was only so much in my head, and I'd spit it all out.

"What about the facts, the quotes?"

"I'm tired of shouting useless citations until my mouth goes dry and my throat starts aching"

"What about your speeches?" El was pressing now.

"There's no point if no one will hear them."

Silence.

"No one but you, of course, but that isn't enough." I felt bad, all of a sudden.

More silence.

"It's just so difficult, El. Life is nothing if I'm not working or dreaming or helping. I need to work, to advance."

The speaker clicked off, though I knew El's shift was far from over. It had been too much, I supposed, all of my confessions. They had driven my only confidant away. I sunk down, my face laid against the floor.

I closed my eyes, exhausted, and faded into darkness.

The dark was enveloping, stifling, twisting into the room's heavy silence. It wasn't like the darkness or the quiet in the mines, its force a dozen hands pressing into my back. It brought to mind memories of waking up from a suffocating nightmare with my face pressed into my pillow. Waves of cold rolled over me, pressing icy fingers into my skin. My breath caught behind my teeth, and I sat up, pressing my knees to my chest. Allowed myself a bit of self pity, a luxurious second of grief for myself before the darkness swallowed me whole.

Then, a window opened in the nothingness. Not a metaphorical, mental window, but the actual, physical window that was set in about the middle of the door. It creaked slightly, a rectangular sliver of slightly brighter fluorescence. With a thump, a paper-bound manual hit the floor. I rose to my feet, grabbing the book. It was yellow and was laminated in shiny plastic, big black letters cheerfully spelling out "PRISON PSYCHOLOGY." I flipped it around in my hands, thoughtfully. It was something to read at least. I looked up at the speaker.

"You give me this and ask me *not* to start a riot?"

Nervous silence.

"I'm not going to start a riot, El."

Crackle.

"I'm not dangerous."

"Don't go about saying that. I've gotten this to you by saying you'd be more dangerous with time to think, and to scheme." El seemed a little excited, though I couldn't tell for certain.

"You told people that I scheme? *Scheme?*"

A quiet "No."

I laughed, which was an uncontrollable, but not at all unpleasant, reaction. My legs were crossed under me and the book laid open in my lap. The spine cracked, and I settled in, my back aching just a little as the ribbed scars were pressed into my skin by the wall. I shifted uncomfortably, half listening to the faint crackling of the speaker that shielded me from the knives hovering an inch above my skull. I read until the room went silent again, and then I kept reading. I'd gone through all of the interesting bits of manual a time and a half by time El opened the window again. I drew over to it, my curiosity piqued.

Another book thumped onto the floor, flipping open and sending something flying across the room. I dealt with that first, finding a blue wax crayon laying in the corner. I knelt by the door and picked up the book, a cheap composition notebook, with the tag half peeled from the back. I found myself absentmindedly flipping it over, front to back to front to back.

"What is this?"

"I picked it up on my way to work. It was a little bit of searching, but couldn't exactly get you a tablet. The crayon is so you can't make a weapon, because that's pretty important to me, but you can write if you'd like to. It's a little more permanent that way, so the speeches aren't just for me to hear. That would be a waste of your words." I couldn't tell if El was upset or intending to make me feel guilty, but I didn't think so.

I bit my cheek to contain the true width of my smile, because if I allowed my joy to be properly drawn out, I wouldn't have known how to act.

The speaker clicked off. Then, I cracked the cover open. On the first page, in black pen "PAGE SIXTEEN"

And on page sixteen, in the same square letters;

"I think you're interesting", with the last word crossed out and replaced with "exceptional", "smart", and finally "onto something." Underneath, El had written "Please talk more about **Why.**"

I tapped the crayon against the paper, hesitating. And then, as I started to write, I spoke too. I rambled about the kids in the tribe, the way they'd supported me as I stitched myself together, the way they acted and felt and how I couldn't disappoint them.

Halfway through, I ripped out the page I'd been writing on, and dropped it by the slot with a soft knock against the metal door. On it, as clearly as I could write;

"Why do you want to know?"

There were a lot of Whys flying around, it seemed. I thought I could assume the answer; El thought I was silly and wanted to know why I'd risk so much. People had questioned it before. But as the paper was slid back in, near the end of my monologue, that wasn't what it said.

"I don't think I've ever seen someone care about any cause so much. I want to care about it."

I paused as I read the paper, the words catching. Instead of continuing, I launched into talking about the books I'd read in the colony, which was something I could do mindlessly as I continued to stare at the words.

I finally wrote back "Why are you doing that job, then."

So many Whys.

The response was faster this time;

"Necessity. But I want to do something worth caring about."

After that, I wrote in silence, mainly, though we passed a few more silent notes. The speaker crackled, and it soothed my head. Earlier, El had been sorry that it was just them, but my thoughts screamed that that was enough. My head still pounded, but not so badly, as it was run through with words. Words shielded me. I moved around the room, pacing some. My old bones and old scars ached, seemingly unconvinced that my body was healed.

My hands shook sometimes too, when my fingers had grown heavy and ached too badly, and the crayon sent sharp lines across the page. I wrote with unsteady wax shapes, but I still wrote. The silence evolved, changing from a brutish, intimidating force to a quiet, dignified presence. A few more days were passed this way, with the silence as my uneasy companion.

I was starting to grow bored and restless, and the pages were filling up or had been ripped out and passed. I had been focused on my own devices, ignoring the noises of the hallway and creaking of the window in the door. They had all faded into a familiar background, a tractable pattern of clicks and clunks and far away footsteps and muted shouts.

A change came again in the form of a paper-wrapped package being squeezed through the door and falling onto the ground with a quiet crackling noise. I had only half opened it before the speaker burst alive in an excited cloud of static.

"Have you opened it?" Definitely eager.

"Not yet."

"Hurry up then," the voice ordered, a smile practically audible in the words.

"What's this?" I opened the package, bright fabrics spilling out into my hands.

"Clothes you came in with. Since you weren't arrested properly, you're not being released properly. Don't dawdle either, though, your friend is harassing us. And not just us, probably. We were told to spare no hesitation in getting you out."

I laughed to myself, thinking about Nova. I chose to hurry as was suggested, changing into the clothes. I wanted to leave, and to see my new friend in person, and to see Nova. I found my earbuds in my pocket and forced them into my ears. The buzzing easily clicked on. Comfort chased my headache away, mainly, and the relief brought tears to my eyes.

I left the plain clothes loosely folded on the floor, the prison psychology book placed on top of the pile, and the notebook next to it. I stretched leisurely, admiring the purple and blue-green decorating my shirt. I tied my boot laces carefully, yanking my colorful socks up above the tops. I liked to look at the reminder that I got to choose what I wore. It was an odd, simple sort of happiness, moving under the obvious joy that comes from an ascent into freedom. I shook out my button down, a small metal piece flying off of it. Rolling up my sleeves, I knelt to pluck the shiny pin off the ground.

It was round and silver colored, and raised black letters exclaimed "SUPPORT A.K." It looked machine made, too. I pinned it to my pocket, grabbing my notebook off the floor as the door rattled open. I almost leapt out, burst into the hall with an exuberant cloud biting at my heels. The cloud hardly carried me a step, however, before I hit a wall.

A wall of person. Just a normal, non-wall-shaped person, but a tall and broad shouldered person. I rubbed my face indignantly, taking a step away from the six foot something Asian man in the guard uniform.

"Where's El?" I demanded, my words carefully civil, but bordered with insistence.

He seemed to have some sort of planned speech or something of that kind, but the words shot back into his throat. He peered at his feet, before focusing his gaze on me again as his finger half pointed to his own chest.

"Ellis."

My voice raised half an octave, at least.

"Oh-"

I would have said more, and it seemed like he would have as well, but Nova had dodged around him and jumped at me, wrapping her arms around my shoulders. Her grip tightened around me, an embrace that almost popped my injured arm out of its socket. I didn't mind though, looping my free arm around her shoulders. She released me after a moment, and I swallowed. My throat was dry. She then looked at Ellis, and I ducked down to tie my shoes, my break of contact seeming to release something, like a cork popping out of a bottle. With that, she started rambling. The force of her words were directed at El, Ellis.

"What are you still doing here?" she demanded. "Do you think he's going to break out? He's already free. Or do you think he's going to let everyone else out? With no key? Just go back to your work."

He stepped away from her ferocity, immediately defensive.

"My name is Ellis, Ellis Lawe. I'd really like to step out with you two, I can mention more then."

Nova turned to me, her question laid out on her face. I glanced at Ellis, but I knew I trusted him even before I met his anxious gaze.

I nodded.

Seeming just a little disappointed, she turned to him "Listen, I've had a tough go of it recently, and if I can be blunt with you-" Ellis nodded "Thanks. This seems like a bad idea. Listening to you, I mean."

"That's fair. Really, it is. This is really weird, and kind of intense, but I'm being honest. I don't mean you harm, I talked to Arthur."

Her expression softened and, with a sigh, she nodded.

"Both of you, I guess; car's outside. Got a self-driving one because of the distance. We're almost in Connecticut, you know."

I had not, in fact, known. I nodded anyway, watching her expression change. There were circles under her eyes, and she kept looking at me and then away again..

She kept talking, "I've been sleeping at a friend's place, but I've got some apartments that I'm looking at. A lot of the landlords even offered us discounts, the smaller ones. People who like big companies are *not* big fans of yours. We can find something, I'm sure." She was talking fast, and speeding down the hallway. Ellis and I half-ran to keep up with the speed with which her heels hit the floor, clicking distinctly.

"I-" El began, pausing as Nova whipped around to face him. I understood her apprehension, of course; Rosaline's betrayal must have really hit her. But still, I was taken aback by the intensity of her defense of my ideas, and her defense of me.

"I've got a place around here. It's small, but not a lot of people around, and it's less than a half hour away. You could stay the night while you get everything all set with your apartment. It'll be safe too, for both of you..If you're worried about that." Before Nova could say anything, I jumped in, putting logic above suspicion.

"That would be fantastic, thank you." His face lit up, and he nodded, rattling off the address.

Nova huffed, but seemed to move past it as she slid into the driver's seat. I sat next to her, and Ellis took a place in the backseat. She was talking again, and I was wildly impressed by her ability to move forward, to have a complete plan. My plans were more momentary, less adaptable, mostly internally focused. She could help herself and me, and she had already grown to include Ellis in her ideas.

"We need to get you back into being a model citizen and a model public figure. All legal, all good, all safe," her voice caught, and she brushed a strand of hair from her face with steady fingers. "We now know that we have to be a little more cautious. But, on that note, there's nothing anyone can hold against you. All good."

"Sounds great." I nodded. "However, there's something I have to do that is objectively good, morally right, ethically the only choice." She seemed pleased. "However, it isn't quite up to your legal standards." Her expression immediately dropped into suspicion.

"What?"

"Break someone out of a Union compound."

"WHAT?"

END OF BOOK ONE

Made in United States
North Haven, CT
30 March 2022